Mistaken Identity

When Benjamin Lightstar and his family move into a house previously occupied by undercover officers, his family is mistakenly targeted for a mob hit. When his wife is killed and his son is wounded, the local sheriff's department, NYPD and the FBI all work to prove the mob boss was responsible; so does SII – Securities International, Incorporated – a firm with former military and intelligence personnel who recently hired Benjamin as an operative. "The Company," as it is known, isn't hampered by probable cause affidavits or warrants; they are unhindered in seeking the truth and will use whatever means they can to do justice for one of their own.

Mistaken Identity

<1>

It sounded strange to hear the word applied to him. It had not been so for twenty-four years. Captain Benjamin Lightstar began his naval career during the Persian Gulf War. The naval operation was a diversion as ground troops would flank Iraqi forces from the west. The war ended nearly as quickly as it began.

'Civilian.' The word rang with an unfamiliar air; the structure and organization of a military career brought one a measure of comfort – even if others were trying to have you killed. Benjamin pondered what a civilian life would entail. It's not as if he hadn't planned this; a security analyst job awaited him and arrangements had been made to close on a house in Babylon, New York. The irony of leaving the area of the historical Babylon for a home in a town on Long Island named Babylon did not escape him.

Benjamin Lightstar would be the resident most likely to stand out; his skin was hardened and brown from his service in Kuwait, Somalia, Iraq and Afghanistan. At this time of year – the temperature in January had already plummeted and the sun set early – others in *this* Babylon would bear a pasty comparison to his complexion.

Following the moving van, Benjamin and his wife and young son, Ben Jr., pulled into the driveway of the clapboard two story house. The house had a gabled oval entrance made of stone, and a breezeway leading to a sunroom. In the rear was a greenhouse; Margaret had a green thumb and would be busy shaping the grounds to her own design. Ben Jr. liked the idea of having a bigger room than in the Maryland apartment in which he and his mom lived before dad retired. He was nine and had not had a room large enough to festoon with sports memorabilia; now he would make the room his own. On one of the four walls would be Ravens banners and posters; on another Redskins. A third wall honored the Nationals; the fourth wall was a tribute to the Orioles. Having lived in Maryland his allegiance was torn between Baltimore and Washington, DC.

Security International, Incorporated. SII. The Company, as it was called, gave Benjamin a week to get settled into his house before reporting for work. He would oversee the operations that provided security and protection to the well-heeled of the world and, occasionally, to far flung government operations. Some in The Company provided security for entertainment personalities, a job both envied and dread; there was excitement in being around the famous, but some fans were obsessive and wanted to be possessive of their idols. The security detail tried not to be impolite but sometimes a fan would be hurt. When it happened that a fan was injured by security, the publicity was harshly critical. And this hurt the reputation of The Company. Agents were trained that, unless there was a weapon, they were to use kid gloves. And it always happened that, when a fan *was* hurt, there were charges filed against the fan; the agents' actions were always justified. That is what The Company spokesperson said in those circumstances. Always.

Settling in – putting things in their proper places – took long hours of each day of that pre-work week. In the end Margaret had put her stamp on their home. She even applied tole painting to 'her' room; the place she went to meditate, read her bible and pray. She looked forward to church shopping, to find a place to worship and praise God, and to be strengthened in her faith among fellow Christ-followers. This time seemed as if it were a time of "starting over" inasmuch as she and Benjamin had been apart so much during the last ten years.

Yet, she had no understanding of the nearness of Jesus that waited for her. Very near and very sudden.

<2>

It was Benjamin's first day on the job. After touring the campus and meeting his associates, he was briefed on a detail involving a task force to protect a foreign dignitary at the United Nations. The target of the protection detail was only given at the last moment; the detail was to secure the target as she deplaned at a JFK airport tarmac, herd her into a waiting bullet-proof vehicle, then whisk her to a secure safe house where she would be guarded until she gave an address at the U.N. Security Council. She would depart immediately after her speech. She was to fly in at 11 PM EST. Benjamin was assigned to the team that was to pick up the target at the airport and sit on her until being relieve at 6 AM.

Snow was falling lightly in New York City; the white blanket-like appearance gave the city a fresh, clean look. At this hour there was a bustle of night life activity. Restaurants and theaters were filled. This was the time New York came alive, this City that never sleeps. The lights of Broadway gave a bright shine to the slush along the street. People hurried to their particular night spot.

Things were more urgent with SII's team.

At 9:00 PM, the team was given the information, the exact runway and tarmac area to pick up the target. The team drove their armor plated Chevy Suburbans to

JFK, showed their identification to the guard at the gate and entered the tarmac area. Each team member had been briefed on their area of duty and were posted to their positions by 10:40 PM.

At 11:01 PM, the target's plane touched down and taxied to the designated area. Two team members converged on the ramp that was positioned beside the plane and they ran to the top of the ramp as the door was opened. Three team members extracted her bags. The target and her bags were put into the Suburbans and the team exited JFK at 11:18 PM.

The drive to the safe house was hurried and uneventful. The target was secured and Benjamin and one SII employee took first watch.

The target was instructed to remain clear of windows; she was restless and moved about frequently with many admonitions about being aware of her position in the various rooms. She continually read from her prepared notes, the speech she would give the next morning. The security detail was no less bored than she was. Sitting on a target was not exciting and all that could be done was to find something to break the boredom. Magazines, newspapers, anything to pass time, yet not being too engrossed by anything. Protecting the target was everything.

Being relieved the following morning, Benjamin left for home. It felt good to be in the morning air; the cold air invigorated him, yet he would soon be drained of emotion and energy.

A meeting had taken place a week before Mr. and Mrs. Benjamin Lightstar and family moved into their Babylon, NY home.

From his cell at Riker's Island Toreo Futcelli was being interviewed by his attorney, William Gambuchi, esquire, in preparation for his pending trial. He – Futcelli - was arrested in a joint FBI/NYPD/Suffolk County Sheriff's raid. The Futcelli family was the subject of an undercover operation that had been months in the making. Gambuchi was the 'Family' attorney of record. He had, without fail, won not guilty verdicts for his clients. These, after witnesses either recanted grand jury testimony or simply failed to show at trial. Today's meeting was a different strategy session. Busted as a result of the undercover sting, Mr. Futcelli wanted more than a not guilty verdict, he wanted revenge on the cop that put him behind bars. He had trusted this man that betrayed him and, now, he wanted him dead.

"You find him! You tell my men where to find him! I want this person done! Am I not making myself understood?"

"Mr. Futcelli, finding an undercover cop is no small thing. The cops, they protect the identity of these people. This won't be easy."

"We've got people on the inside. I don't care what it takes, how much it costs. Find him!"

"Yes sir, Mr. Futcelli."

"And when you find him, I want him dead! Do you understand me?"

"Yes, sir."

"What?"

"Yes, sir. Mr. Futcelli."

"Get outa here. Get this done!"

After that meeting began a search. The search would bring two different worlds on a collision course. Three worlds: law enforcement from the Suffolk County Sheriff's Department, NYPD, FBI and the U.S. Southern District of New York; the underworld; and a security company that had a reach as long – if not longer – than all the others combined, and was unrestrained by any legal impediments.

<4>

When the informant found the information a call was made.

"Mr. Gambuchi, you have a call on line two."

"Thanks, Maria."

Picking up the phone, he knew the nature of the call. It would be signal to make a call from a throw-away phone to a number he knew by heart, another throw-away.

"Hello. This is Mr. Gambuchi."

"Ya know, I, ah, think I have the wrong number. Is this Salvatore's Flower Shop?"

"No. You have the wrong number."

They broke off the call and William Gambuchi pulled the throw-away phone from his bottom desk drawer. He flipped open the phone then dialed the number.

"Yeah, Mr. G?"

"Yes. What can you tell me?"

"Cop's name is Clete Decker. Lives in Babylon."

The attorney was given the address. He hung up and buzzed his secretary.

"I'll be out of the office awhile. If anyone calls, take messages and I'll deal with them when I get back."

"Yes, Mr. Gambuchi."

Putting on his coat and hat, he made his way to the street and hailed a cab. He ordered the cabby to take him uptown, got out, and hailed another cab to take him to his destination in Long Island City.

"Is he in," he asked as he walked in?

"In his office," the bartender stated. "He's waiting for you."

Walking in, William Gambuchi handed the man a note, turned and left. He caught a cab back to his office.

This place, the place in which Gambuchi handed over the information, was what in common parlance is known as a "gentlemen's club," a euphemism for a strip joint. The Red Garter was a one story building with a brightly lit marquee that featured a statue of a woman in underwear and one red garter on her right thigh. The busy street led to the open parking lot on the east side of the building.

<5>

While Benjamin and his team were guarding the safe house and nearing the time they were to be relieved, his home was being broken into.

The alarm was disabled and the patio door was jimmied. Three men in masks slipped in and made their way to the back bedroom. She made a small whine as the bullet entered her chest, then made no more noise as the second bullet entered her skull squarely in the center of her forehead.

The search for a male occupant turned up nothing. The young boy appeared in the hallway, yawning and adjusting his eyes to the darkened environment. One bullet put him on the floor. His assailant stood over him and, thinking him dead, left him lie there.

When Benjamin returned home from his shift, he was disturbed when he saw the alarm keypad was not lighted; something was wrong. He rushed to hallway and turned on the light. The sight of his son on the floor brought a new rush of adrenalin. There was a small pool of blood on the floor beside his son.

He dialed 9-1-1 as he entered the bedroom. He froze. On their blood-soaked bed lay Margaret. The empty glazed look in her eyes was haunting. He sat on the floor by their bed and wept. He had dropped the phone on the carpeted floor and didn't hear the

"Military?"

"Seal, sir."

"Thank you for your service. I'm sorry for your loss. Is there anything you can tell me that might help us find who killed your wife and hurt your son?"

"No. I'm...at a loss."

The medical examiner reported to Ricardo that the killing took place between 5:30 and 6:30.

"Did we find any shell casings?" Detective Ricardo said to no one in particular.

"None, sir," came the reply from one of the crime scene techs. "The shooter either used a wheel gun or picked up the shell casings."

The crime scene supervisor reported no fingerprints were found by the patio door, on the walls in the hallway or anywhere in the bedroom. They were still searching for fiber evidence.

During subsequent interviews with Benjamin's supervisor to inquire about his whereabouts, his alibi was confirmed. It would be impossible for Benjamin to be in Babylon any sooner than 7:15-7:30.

<6>

At the hospital, Benjamin could do no more than wait. His SII supervisor stayed with him and gave him assurances that The Company would begin their own investigation into the slaying of his wife.

At 4:10 PM the surgeon came and reported on Ben Jr.'s progress.

"The wound was a through and through but tore up some muscle. He's stable. He will recover. With some therapy he will be fine. I'm very sorry to hear of your wife's death."

Detective Ricardo came from the entrance with another detective in tow.

"Doctor, can we interview the boy? We have some questions for him. Should only take five minutes."

"I'm sorry, but he is sedated; he will be unavailable the rest of the day."

"It's important that we speak to him."

"You can speak to him, but not now. Not today."

"Hmph." Ignoring the doctor, he turned to Benjamin. "We have nothing right now, sir. Except for how your son was shot, this looks like a mob hit. They usually do a thorough job and don't leave anyone behind who can identify them. Your son was lucky."

"Lucky? He only lost his mother. Is that what you mean by 'lucky'?"

"No. No, sir. I didn't mean that at all. I can't imagine your grief. I'm sorry. We'll be back tomorrow."

Once the detectives left, the doctor spoke. "He's awake and wants to see you."

"I'll wait in the hall," Bill Sturgeon, his SII supervisor said.

"No. Please. Come in with me."

As they entered the room the boy lay lifeless and pale on the bed. But his eyes, through tears, opened wide when he saw his father. He lifted the oxygen masked and sobbed, "Oh, dad! What happened?" "Where's mom?"

"Your mom couldn't come, son. Can you tell me what happened?"

Taking a series of deep breaths, Ben Jr. told what he saw and heard. "I heard a sound. Like a yelp or a gasp. A noise. I woke up and got out of bed. When I went to see what the noise was, something hit me in the side; it hurt and I fell down. A man stood over me; he was wearing a mask so I couldn't see his face. I saw a mark, a tattoo, on the back of his hand though. I don't know what it was, but it had a heart on it and a banner with some writing. Oh, and a woman – she had three legs, one going in front to one side, one going in front to the other side and one in back. The writing was something like 'con tott mio coro' or something like that."

Bill had been taking notes while Ben Jr. told them what had happened. It didn't make sense that someone would take out the family. There was no reason for it.

"Get some rest son. I'll stay here with you," Ben told him.

"I want to check some things for you," Bill said and left.

Back at The Company, Bill called in one of his intelligence operatives and briefed him. He was tasked with finding anything that could be found about what happened and about the tattoo.

The operative had a file on Benjamin that had been vetted before his hire. Nothing would be found there. Ben's work in the gulf left no one who would be able to extract vengeance for his work there. But what? The neighborhood? It was an upper middle class neighborhood. A search of Suffolk County police files proved this area to be a low – very low – crime area. The house? Examining the abstract he found a turnover in ownership about every three years. He noted the names: Jimmy Vasco was listed as owner before Benjamin Lightstar; before that, Juan Pedro Torreli; and before that Anthony Jackson. The rapid turnover was odd. The average in America is about eight years; this house in Babylon had a rate of less than three years.

When he accessed the criminal files of the Suffolk County Sheriff's Department he found each of these names. They were listed in the criminal database with various offenses, including armed robbery, racketeering and assault. Each file had offenses that predated the creation of the file by years, sometimes decades. These weren't a record of criminal activity; these were created to give bonafides to an undercover cop. In each case, the files were accessed soon after the Babylon property was put into the name of the 'criminal.' Each UC took possession of the house in Babylon and, soon after, the file was accessed.

Examining case files he was able to find a pattern. He looked for files that were closed at the same time the Babylon property changed owners. Cross referencing the closed files to major criminal prosecutions created a pattern: new owner, criminal file access; case file closed, major prosecution; another new owner. The last major prosecution? Toreo Futcelli. But who was Jimmy Vasco? Who was the UC and how did the hit team know where to find him?

He found accounting files in the SCSD database. Police personnel received their pay on a regular basis; UC's didn't stop in to pick up their checks and the checks wouldn't be mailed to their operational house. Their handlers provided cash with which to operate, but their checks would be sequestered into an internal account. There were accounts of this type going back over a decade. It was a simple matter to match the dates these files were closed to the three prior owners of the Babylon house. The last of which was Clete Decker, on loan from the NYPD. These UC's were often not locals as an identification of an undercover officer by a former acquaintance would blow a case and cause the death of the UC. Clete Decker was Jimmy Vasco.

Finding the mole became much easier. The user name and password used to access the files when the undercover ops began was the same as that used to access the Decker file: SCSD clerk Amanda Vicardo.

Now that he had pieced together the information of the former resident and the mole, the intelligence operative began searching for the meaning of the tattoo. A woman's head. Three legs. A heart and the inscription on the banner. He called a friend.

Benny was a former Green Beret. Fought in Viet Nam. Came home and became a tattoo artist. His loves were his bike, tattooing, and opera.

"Yeah. Benny."

"Benny, this is Clarence Thomas. Howz it?" Clarence had worked in counter intelligence at CIA. Prior to his stint there, he was Naval Intelligence. He may be the best hacker in the world – better than the Russians or the Chinese; while *they* were hacking us, he was in their systems watching.

"Man, I haven't heard from you in a while. Thought you might be dead."

"I'm alive. Hey, I need your help. I'm trying to identify a tattoo from a description of a witness."

"The Babylon hit?"

"Yeah, the Babylon hit. Anyway, a witness says he saw a tattoo of a woman with three legs, a heart and a banner with some writing on it."

"Con Tutto il Mio Cuori. 'With all my heart.' It's called Trinacria. The woman is Medusa. It's a symbol of Sicily. Gimme your email and I'll send it to you. Check out the flag of Sicily; it's on there, too."

Ten minutes later Clarence had a print out of Trinacria and was headed to Bill's office.

"Sir, I think I've put together some of what happened this morning."

"Sit down, Clarence. Tell me what you've got."

"It was a hit. The target was an undercover cop. The house had been used as the cop's place before Benjamin bought it. The abstract had multiple owners in short succession, but, until Benjamin bought the house, it was used by the Suffolk County Sheriff's Department as a base for undercover operations. The last owner was listed as Jimmy Vasco, an alias for NYPD officer Clete Decker. He was working on a case that recently closed; Toreo Futcelli was the target. He's on Riker's Island awaiting trial"

"Ok. What about the tattoo Ben Jr. saw? What's that?"

"Sicilian, sir. It's called Trinacria. Here it is." Clarence handed the print-out to Bill.

"Thanks. I'm headed to the hospital."

On his way to the elevator, Bill called Benjamin.

"This is Ben.."
"Benjamin, listen. I have some information to share with you. Meet me at the hospital."
"I'm at the hospital. With Ben. What is it?"

"It can wait until I get there. We're making some progress."

<8>

"Is he awake," Bill whispered?

"I'm awake," Ben Jr. said.

"Ben, I want to show you something; a picture. Tell me if you recognize it.

When Ben was shown the picture, his eyes grew huge. "That's it! That's the tattoo the man had! Did you find him?"

"No, Ben, but were getting close. I need to talk with your dad for a moment – in private. He won't be gone long."
"Ok. Thanks, dad, for being with me."

"I love you, son. I'll be right back."

In the hall, Bill explained what they found, that the house had been used by SCSD in an undercover operation and that the hit was made because the mob thought the cop still was there.

"Keep me in the loop. Thanks for what you're doing."

"Our intelligence analyst has uncovered the information we have so far; he's found the identity of the UC. We know the case he was working on and think we know who ordered the hit. We'll handle that any way you want; we can hand it over to the police or...whatever you want."

"I'm too broken to make that decision right now. I'm all about getting Ben healed physically and get him the emotional help he's going to need. He doesn't even know about his mother yet."

"You're covered by The Company insurance plan. We'll do everything to help."

"Thanks. Keep me informed."

Clarence Thomas dug deeper into the Futcelli operation. It was typical mob stuff.

Toreo Futcelli worked out of Queens and ran an operation on the North Shore. Drugs and prostitution. Protection racket. A full service operation. Clete was able to infiltrate the racket on the basis of his dummied up criminal record. According to Clete's file, he had been working this case for over two years. The criminal file was created for Decker's benefit and was then accessed by Amanda Vicardo soon after contact was made between Decker and the mob. Clete Decker's record at NYPD was clean; he had received no special awards which kept him below the publicity radar and no reprimands that would have made the newspapers. He had graduated from the academy at the middle of his class in 2008. Nothing about him garnered public attention. A perfect profile for a UC.

A search of visitations to Riker's Island found Toreo Futcelli was visited by William Gambuchi, attorney to the mob. That same afternoon the Decker file was accessed by Amanda Vicardo. Clarence searched phone records of Ms. Vicardo's work station telephone and found one call made to the office of William Gambuchi. The call was less than ten seconds long, long enough to signal a call that was untraceable. Amanda Vicardo was the mole; William Gambuchi passed information to a fixer and the hit was ordered. Only the mob didn't know that Clete Decker had moved and the Benjamin Lightstar and family now occupied the house.

Clarence briefed his boss. His boss called Detective Ricardo and told him some of what he knew. It was divulged that the house was used in a UC operation and that the hit was probably ordered by Futcelli through Gambuchi. Information on Amanda Vicardo was not shared, nor were SII's methods. It was suggested that Detective Ricardo search through the files on Jimmy Vasco and Clete Decker; they would find the link there.

It was quite a dance around how SII had the information and in the end Detective Ricardo simply said, "Never mind. I don't even want to know."

Detective Pedro Ricardo contacted his lieutenant with an update on the case. He waited while the LT made a couple of phone calls.

"Yes, Clete Decker was NYPD working undercover out of the Babylon house. His alias was Jimmy Vasco. The target was the Futcelli family and a major bust took place ten days ago."

"How did Futcelli know about Clete?"

"I don't know, but we have people in Babylon too scared to leave their houses. We have to get in front of this somehow."

"A press briefing?"

"Yes, but it must be carefully worded. We can't prove the criminal connection between Futcelli and Gambuchi – it's circumstantial – so we can't mention names."

"Yes, sir."

That afternoon Detective First Class Pedro Ricardo stood before the microphones with cameras rolling and klieg lights glaring. His countenance was sober.

"I am here to provide an update on the homicide in Babylon. The residence was used by one of our undercover officers. That officer has moved and the house sold to a private citizen. We believe the target of the homicide was the undercover officer. We are doing all we can to uncover the identity of those involved in this gruesome act. Thank you. I will *not* take questions."

With that Detective Ricardo went inside. He leaned against a wall and sighed. He felt overwhelmed. This was much, much different than any case he had handled. There were unanswered questions. He knew that there had to be an information source within his department that provided intelligence to Futcelli's people. He didn't know how to find that link. Until he could find out, he trusted very few people within SCSD.

"Gambuchi contacts someone in Futcelli's operation. Who? Was the contact made in person? Phone? Was the phone traceable?" Clarence played these over in his mind. It's one of those problems that leads one to propose ideas, then scrutinize each one to find the answers.

Phone records of Gambuchi's home, office and cell phones turned up no calls to Futcelli's people. Gambuchi had a driver, but sometimes traveled by taxi. Hacking the computers of the driving service turned up no travel by the service during the week in question. One thing interesting did turn up though. Credit card receipts on that Thursday showed the attorney travelling uptown, then switched cabs for Queens. He was let off at a gentlemen's club, The Red Garter. He took a cab from the club back to his office fifteen minutes later.

The gentlemen's club in Queens was a known base of prostitution. From time to time the women and/or the johns were arrested, but the operation continued mostly unabated. The women were usually young and from out of town. Welcome to New York City, ladies. The clientele varied depending on the day and the time of day; working class guys during the afternoon, the smooth, well-coiffed after dark. The object was the same: pry some money out of the hands of the clients.

The information on the club was passed on to his boss who put one of the company investigators to the task of finding out about the visit to the gentlemen's club.

<12>

Agent Reynolds was tall – six foot, seven inches – and a trained black belt. Trained in the Marines, he had served well and was given a citation of valor when he had carried three of his buddies on his back for three miles to safety in Fallujah in Anbar Province, Iraq. He looked intimidating in his athletic shirt and khaki pants, wearing combat boots. Not always his attire, this was worn for its intimidation quotient.

As he entered the club, he stopped and surveyed the interior. He saw mostly urban working class folks and a few women in enticing attire. The man he was interested in turned and went into a back room. Reynolds walked at a casual pace to the end of the bar near the office. When he got to the door, two men appeared there to block his way. Behind the men, sitting at a desk was a well-dressed man with slicked back black hair. Since the men were standing in the doorway it was no large task to splinter the door jamb with each man's head. Reynolds stepped over them as they slumped to the floor. As he entered the room, the bartender appeared behind him with a shotgun. Reynolds' spin-kick sent the shotgun flying. He broke the bartender's arm with one blow, then put him out with a blow to the carotid.

The man behind the desk had backed himself into a wall. Fear covered his face and he was visibly trembling. Reynolds took the man by the neck and politely inquired about Mr. Gambuchi's previous visit.

"Gambuchi? Gambuchi? I don't know any Gambuchi!" the man replied.

"How about now?" Reynolds asked, tightening his grip.

"I'm not afraid of you. I know people who will do more to me than you can if I talk."

"Let's see." Dragging him to the bathroom, Reynolds grabbed a hand towel, laid the man on his back and began to shovel handfuls of water over his towel-draped face. The man coughed and sputtered.

"Are you feeling chatty now?"

"No! I'm not talking."

More water. Then more water. Then some more.

"Stop! Stop! I'll talk!"

"Tell me what you know about Gambuchi."

"He came in here last Thursday and gave me a note. I didn't read it; I passed it to Freddy Batamata."

"Who is Freddy Batamata?"

"He's one of Futcelli's men. He's a made man, I hear. Lots of kills."

"How do I find him?"

"Find him? He should be here by now."

"What's he look like?"

"Italian! That's what he looks like. Havanera chambray shirt, Chino's and dress shoes. And a leather jacket! Slicked back black hair. Clean shaven."

"Get up."

The man stood and Reynolds knocked him out.

"That should take care of you for a while."

Reynolds placed a bug in the office, dragged the two men from the doorway into the office and shut the door.

As Reynolds walked toward the front door, Freddy walked in. Reynolds knocked him out with a single blow to the forehead and carried him to his car.

<13>

The fogginess subsided as Freddy Batamata comes to. His hands are tied behind him and his feet are secured to the chair legs.

"Hello, Freddy. I have a few questions. I expect your full cooperation."

Struggling with the cords that bind him he replies, "Whataya nuts! Do you know who I am? You'll burn for this!"

"Now that's not the cooperation I had hoped for. Let me just get to the part where I demonstrate my insistence on getting from you what I want."

Reynolds kicked the chair and Freddy went over backwards. The jolt to his head almost put him out again.

Just as he was about to scream obscenities at Reynolds, a towel was put over his face and water was poured on his head. For nearly a minute water was poured over his head. Freddy was gagging and coughing. Then it stopped.

"I will do more if you don't cooperate."

"Fu.."

More water.

"Stop! What. Do. You. Want?" he sputtered.

"You were handed a note from William Gambuchi with the name and address of an undercover cop. What did you do with the note?"

"What do you care?"

The towel. The water. More sputtering from Batamata.

"I, I p-planned a, ah h-hit with, with some... of my boys."

"And you did this hit? In Babylon?"
"Yeah."

"And where can I find these men of yours?"

"Hey, pal, it's your funeral. They hang out at the club. The one you grabbed me at. They're bodyguards there."

"We've met. Thanks."

With a single twist on Batamata's neck, he went limp. Reaching down, Reynolds inspected Batamata's hands. On the back of his right hand was the Trinacria tattoo.

"Nice ink," Reynolds said to a dead Freddy Batamata.

On Riker's Island Toreo Futcelli was meeting with his attorney.

"What the hell happened out there? Who the hell is this woman that was killed?"

"Mr. Futcelli, I got the information on the house and passed it on. How was I to know it was the wrong people there?"

"I got a bunch of idiots workin' for me! You better take care of this! Clean it up! Whatever it takes. Bring in my people from Baltimore! Fix it!"

"Yes, sir, Mr. Futcelli."

"And another thing, make sure the doers get gone. And I don't care where. Out of the country!"

"Yes, sir."

"Damned idiots," he muttered, "I could have another indictment on my hands over this. Stupid!"

Gambuchi didn't hear the last of this commentary as he was already gone. But Gambuchi didn't know how tight the noose was – or how much tighter it would become.

<15>

Dressed in a cashmere overcoat and gray bowler hat, William Gambuchi exited the cab in front his office; he didn't notice the black Tahoe. He didn't notice until two men approached and, grabbing him by his elbows, herded him into the waiting vehicle. A bag was placed over his head and, hearing, feeling the blow to his temple, he slumped over in the seat.

When he awoke he was tied to a chair, the bag still on his head. He couldn't see, but he heard the voice of his interlocutor.

"Mr. Gambuchi, did Toreo Futcelli give the order to execute Clete Decker?"

"That's attorney-client privilege. Any conversations I had with Mr. Futcelli is confidential. I can't talk about it."

The jolt from the Taser knocked Mr. Gambuchi into unconsciousness. The pain was still gripping him as he came to. "What the…" He was zapped again. He awakened, but more slowly this time.

"Who ordered the hit?"

"I can't…"

The utterance was interrupted by the buzzing of the Taser. Before it could come into contact, Gambuchi gave up all he knew.

"Yes! Yes! Futcelli gave the order!"

"And how did you find the cop's identity?"

"What?"

"Mr. Gambuchi, need I Taser you again?"

"No! Please! Futcelli has an informant at SCSD. Name's Vicardo. Amanda Vicardo! She's in records and has access to all the files in the SCSD system."

"How does she contact you?"

"She calls my office...I tell her it's a wrong number. After we hang up, I call her on a throw away phone. It's untraceable."

"Very good. How did you get this to Futcelli's people?"

"I call them."

Gambuchi passes out again from the Taser. When he awakes, the question is answered.

"I took a note to a club in Queens. It's a strip joint in Long Island City. The Red Garter. I gave it to the guy in the back."

"Mr. Gambuchi, thank you for your cooperation. Here's what's going to happen. You will be driven to a place in the city and let go. You will find your way back to your office. Do not call Ms. Vicardo and warn her; it is too late for that. She is being held for questioning as we speak. The information we have, information you corroborated will be handed over to the SCSD and you will be charged as an accomplice to a murder-for-hire; a capital offense. Mr. Futcelli will also be charged with this offense. Do not warn Futcelli.

With that two men untied him and took Mr. Gambuchi to midtown Manhattan, deposited him on a street corner and sped away.

In another room, Amanda Vicardo gave up the same information, much more willingly that did Mr. Gambuchi. She too was informed of her legal fate and dumped at the campus of NYU Stony Brook.

The information obtained would be of no forensic use as the techniques were, well, improper. Neither Gambuchi nor Vicardo knew this. Gambuchi was clearly terrified, too terrified to think as an attorney would have about this evidence gathering; Vicardo wasn't smart enough to be afraid.

Benjamin Lightstar would be given the option of how to proceed.

<16>

A knock disturbed his train of thought.

"Come in."

A large man with dark skin and a scruffy moustache entered carrying a manila folder.

"Forensics report, sir. She was killed with the second bullet, but the coroner says she would have died within minutes from the first bullet. Nine mil, hollow point; the bullets exploded upon impact."

"How do you know first bullet, second bullet?"

"There was little bleeding from the head wound because the vic's blood pressure had drastically dropped from the chest wound. The first wound was the bleeder, the chest wound."

"Thank you, sergeant. Is there any information of the crime scene people?"

"Yes, sir. No prints and no fiber. The doers did a good job of not leaving any evidence."

"Thanks. Get me one of our computer guys ASAP."
"Yes, sir."

With that the sergeant exited and Detective Ricardo opened the file. The vic was asleep when attacked and there was no sign of a struggle. There was nothing under her nails and no blood splatter from the wounds. The first shot caused bleeding, but because the vic was on her back on the bed, the blood soaked into the mattress. The second shot produced only minimal spray as the blood pressure had dropped due to the first wound.

A rapping at the door startled him; he had so focused on the forensics report.

"Come in!"

The door opened and a young bespectacled man in a dress shirt and bow tie entered.

"I'm Jimmy from the computer lab, sir. You wanted to see me?" Jimmy said in a high pitched voice.

"Jimmy, we're working the Lightstar homicide. Somehow SII found the connection to the house our UC was using. I want you to find that link too."

"SII, sir? UC? I don't know these things, sir."

"SII is short for Security International, Incorporated, the company at which Benjamin Lightstar, the vic's...victim's husband worked. UC is short for 'Undercover Cop'. Somehow they got the information from our files. I want to know how."

"Oh, I can tell you that, sir. You see our servers are porous. I think anybody could hack into our network," he snickered.

"What? We're the sheriff's department! We should be secure!"

"Well, sir, I've been trying to get the county to authorize funding to upgrade and secure our network. They reject it because they haven't the funds to do it."

"Is there any way we can trace the hack?"

"Only if they're amateurish, sir; if they're professionals like I imagine Security…er, SII to be, they probably left no trace. But I'll check. Which files were they?"

"One of the files was a criminal file: Jimmy Vasco; the other was investigative file named Clete Decker."

Jimmy scribbles the names on a note pad. "I'll check the files, sir."

"Get back to me…soon! Very soon!"

"Yes, sir! Roger! Wilco! Out!"

"You. Out!"

"Yes, sir." And he left.

<17>

Amanda Vicardo left the SCSD headquarters at 4:30 PM. She got into her Audi A3 and drove through Islip. She pulled into the parking lot of Maxwell's, parked and went inside. She found the gentleman seated at a table near the kitchen and sat beside him so their conversation would not be overheard. The drink was already in front of her place setting. A Manhattan, what else? Close enough to New York City.

"They know about the hit and they're looking for the leaker. What do you plan to do?" he asked.

How she longed for the days before restaurants went 'no smoking.' She desperately wanted a smoke. She looked around, seeing the happy hour crowd arriving.

"Somebody grabbed me yesterday. They know about me already. It wasn't the cops though."

"How do you know it wasn't the cops?"

"Cops don't put hoods over your face when they interrogate you."

"Well, somehow the cops figured out the target of the hit. That means they know the alias and they know the identity of the cop." His voice began to rise and he had to check himself. He quickly glanced around the room to see if he had attracted anyone's attention.

The crowd was busy with their drinks and talking Giants football.

"I don't know what to do. This wasn't supposed to get out of hand like this."

"I suggest you make serious vacation plans before the cops nail you. Permanent vacation plans. It's only a matter of time before the cops finger you!"

"If I go, they'll know for sure it was me!"

"Keep your voice down."

"Look, if I go, they will know. I can't go. I won't go."

"Have it your way."

She finished her drink, got up and left.

He made a phone call and gave the order.

She made her way along 27A past Bay Shore when her car was bumped from behind. Panicked, she sped up. Driving around and between the cars, she was exceeding eighty miles per hour. As she rounded a sharp corner, she lost control. The car overturned and slammed into a utility pole. The gas tank had ruptured. The pursuing car stopped briefly, the passenger side window was rolled down and a lit cigar was tossed on the ground near the car.

In the rear view mirror, the scene was an inferno.

The police might make the connection, but no information would be gotten from Amanda Vicardo.

Detective First Class Pedro Ricardo's phone rang.

"Ricardo, where are we at on the Babylon murder?"

"LT, we are certain the murder was ordered by Futcelli; Gambuchi was probably the conduit to Futcelli's people. We don't know the mole yet."

"Well, I think that's changed."

"How so?"

"There was a crash last night on the 27A. A silver Audi A3 driven by Amanda Vicardo."

"Who is Amanda Vicardo?"

"She's a clerk for SCSD. She has access to all our records. I need you to check – see if she's the mole."

"I'll get the computer geek on it. He's checking on the possibility that SII hacked into our network."

"Wait. What? Isn't our network secure?"

"Not according to the geek. Say's he tried getting money to upgrade our system and make it secure but the board wouldn't approve the funds."

"Hang on. I'm writing this down. I bowl with two of the board members; I'll rattle their chain and get this approved posthaste! You, find out about Vicardo!

Oh, and find out how a clerk with SCSD can afford an A3!"

"Yes, sir. I'm on it."

Hanging up, he buzzed his computer technician.

"Yeah, boss."

Detective Ricardo heard some snorting sounds in his ear. "What the hell is that noise?"

"Sorry, boss. I'm eating a sandwich."

"That's the noisiest sandwich I've ever heard."

"It's the lettuce, sir. Very crisp."

"Very. Look there was an accident on the 27A last night. The driver was Amanda Vicardo. She's a clerk with SCSD and I need you to check her computer logs relative to Jimmy Vasco/Clete Decker. There's a mole in our offices and I need to know if she is that mole."

"Amanda...how's that last name again?"

"V-i-c-a-r-d-o. Vicardo."

"I have her records. She has logged into criminal records several times in the past decade and, more recently into the case files of Toreo Futcelli."

"You found that out...already?"

"Sure, boss! It's not hard if you know where to look."

"What criminal files was she in?"

"Well, the oldest one was Anthony Jackson, then Juan Pedro Torreli and Jimmy Vasco. The...let's see...hang on, this will take a minute. Yeah, boss. She accessed Clete Decker's file. File says he's a cop with NYPD. Why would we have a file on a cop with NYPD?"

"Too complicated to explain." A computer geek doesn't need to know how undercover operations work. "So she accessed all those files. Thanks."

"Sure thing, boss."

They broke off and Detective Ricardo called his LT.

"Boss, Amanda Vicardo accessed files on Jimmy Vasco, which we knew about; Anthony Jackson and Juan Pedro Torreli. These were criminal files. Also the personnel file of Clete Decker. Who is Jackson and Torreli? If Jimmy Vasco was an alias for a UC, was Jackson and Torreli aliases?"

"Check with Willy Jeorgeson. He runs the UC ops. He'll know." The 'J' was pronounced like a 'Y.' 'Yorg-a-son'

A call to Willy Jeorgeson was answered by a man with a thick Nordic accent.

"Vaat?" Willy Jeorgeson asked.

"Willy Jeorgeson?"

"Yeah. I am Willy Jeorgeson. Vaat you vant?"

"Detective Ricardo here. I'm working on the Babylon case. Files for Jimmy Vasco, an alias for Clete Decker working out of the house on Long Island, was accessed by one of our clerks. She also accessed criminal files on Anthony Jackson and Juan Pedro Torreli. Were those also aliases?"

"Und who vants to know?"

"I'm Detective First Class Pedro Ricardo of Homicide. I'm working a murder case out of Babylon.

"Oh, sure. I know dat one. Vait. I vil see."

Silence. A very long silence, but Pedro could hear file drawers being opened and shut. He then heard the sound on the phone's receiver hitting something and making a noise so loud that Pedro quickly moved the phone away from his ear.

"I got files now. Bot men be undercover alias."

William Gambuchi sat at his office desk, top right hand drawer open and the gun visible. The thought that he could not exonerate Toreo Futcelli haunted him. More than that, he was caught between two big fish: the law and Futcelli. He could be indicted for a capital offense and face a possible death sentence or Futcelli could have him killed.

Through the course of the day, he refused to take phone calls and handled the gun dozens of times.

He knew that, because of attorney client privilege he could not testify against Futcelli. Except. Except for his part in the Babylon killing. He realized that he was acting not as Futcelli's attorney, but rather as an accomplice. He certainly could go to the police with that and make a plea agreement; the cops would readily take that, wouldn't they?

As the day wore on and the sun began to set, the darkness outside cast a pall over his office. He truly did not know what to do.

He left his office and went to a nearby club.

As he sat down and took the first taste of his martini a man sat next to him.

"Mr. Gambuchi, right?"

"Look, leave me alone. This has not been a good day for me."

"Well, now. That's too bad. Mr. Futcelli asked me to visit you. Wants to know how you're doing with his problem."

"I'm working on it. I'm working on it!"

"Hey, no need to shout. Mr. Futcelli is worried you can't do for him what he wants done. Is that the problem? You can't do this thing for him?"

"Yes. No. I don't know. Tell Mr. Futcelli, I'm workin' on it."

"Sure thing, Mr. Gambuchi. I hope things go well for you. I hope you keep your health."

With that the man left. The lawyer had never seen the man before and had no idea who he was but was certain that if Futcelli wanted to reach out to him, he would have no problem doing so. Gambuchi realized he was as good as dead.

He left and took a cab home. He noticed an unmarked car tailing him.

20

In the morning, waiting for his car outside his brownstone he saw him. Same guy. Sitting in a car down the street from him. Then something else. Another car was parked in the other block. If the one guy was Futcelli's man, then the other must be...a cop?

Gambuchi was feeling more pressure now. As if things couldn't get worse, the car – not Futcelli's guy, the other one – pulled up blocking his ride. Two men got out of the car.

"William Gambuchi, I'm Detective Williams of NYPD, this is Sergeant James. We request the presence of your company at the precinct. There are some questions we need to ask."

"I'm an attorney. Unless I am under arrest I'm not going with you."

"See that car down there?" Sergeant James asked. "That's Mickey Zeno. He's one of Futcelli's men sent to watch you. He's concerned – Futcelli's concerned – that you might turn on him. And we're just having this chat with you, here on the street. If I were to, I don't know, thank you for your help and cooperation, what would Zeno think of that? It would actually be a good thing if you would come with us."

"You're gonna get me killed talkin' like that."

"My partner's methods are a little intimidating at times. I apologize for him. He just goes off like that sometimes and I can't do anything about it. What do you say? Hop in the car."

Gambuchi got in the car.

<21>

The car pulled into the parking area of Midtown North Precinct and William Gambuchi was escorted to an interrogation room. In spite of its location in Manhattan the inside of the interrogation room was drab; its walls gray and the room decorated by a lone table, four chairs and a one way mirror. Gambuchi was sweating. Escorted to a chair facing the one way mirror, he dropped heavily onto it. His countenance was of one who was already beaten.

"Can I get you anything?" asked Sergeant James. "Some water? Coffee?"

"Water. Please. I'd like some water."

Directly an officer entered with a paper cup filled with water and handed it to Sergeant James.

"Here's some water. Thank you for your willingness to come here. We appreciate it."

"I'm not willing. It's come here or face...what's his name?"

"Mickey Zeno."

"Yeah. Anyway, I don't know what I can disclose to you that would not violate attorney-client privilege."

Before we begin, I want you to understand that you do not have to talk to us and that you can request a lawyer if you choose. Do you understand these rights?

"I'm…yeah. I understand."

"Well, William, the thing is that it is possible you conspired with Toreo Futcelli in a criminal act. Anything along those lines – hypothetically – is not covered by privilege. We believe we have ample evidence to indict you on a conspiracy to commit offense, namely a murder-for-hire in the death of Margaret Lightstar in Babylon. Since this was hatched from Ricker's it's within the jurisdiction of the NYPD."

"I, I don't, ah, know what you're talking about."

"Oh, I think you do."

As previously planned, the door opened and an officer handed Detective Williams a piece of paper and whispered to the detective.

"Thank you, officer," Detective Williams said.

"There was a car crash on Long Island last night – an inferno, actually. Killed in the fire was Amanda Vicardo, a clerk with the Suffolk County Sheriff's Department. Suffolk County says they recovered a phone from the wreckage of Amanda Vicardo's car. The last call received was traced to a phone at your office address. The call was made five seconds after a call was made from her office phone at SCSD to your office. The car she was driving was an Audi A3, a very expensive car for a clerk at SCSD…"

"I don't.."

"Please. There's more. We retrieved the VIN number off the engine block of her car and, along with the license plate information, we found the car was owned by an export-import company in Queens. All financials and legal representation for the company are listed in...your name, Mr. Gambuchi. In fact, your signature is on the paperwork for the purchase of the car. Why would your name be listed as the purchaser of her car? What is your relationship to Ms. Vicardo?"

"All right. She's my mistress."

"And how is it you and her carried on a relationship? If we check with your driving service will we find any trace that you were driven anywhere that might be a rendezvous? Will we be able to check your credit card purchases to find hotel receipts? Restaurant receipts? Cab fare receipts?"

Sergeant James interjected, "You see, it was your credit that was used to take a taxi uptown where you got out, hailed another cab to take you to Long Island City, to a strip club. Yeah, we know about that!"

"You're in a squeeze," Williams said.

Gambuchi was in a panic. His head hung down. He clutched his face.

Williams again, "You can talk to us and maybe make a deal for yourself..."

"Or you can talk to Mickey," James shouted, slamming his hand on the table.

"There is no way you get away free. We can talk to the DA and maybe – just maybe – get you in a witness protection program. Who knows, life at a Gap store in Cheyenne ought to be better that a needle…"

"Or a bullet from Mickey!"

"There's no execution in New York!"

"So the case gets handed off to the feds; they *do* have capital punishment. You're involved with organized crime – which has tentacles that cross state lines. That makes it fall under the jurisdiction of the feds. Got it?" James said. James was so close he could smell Gambuchi's breath and Gambuchi's face was dripping with sweat.

"Wait! No! I need to think about this. I'm not making a deal yet. You want Futcelli bad and you'll make the deal tomorrow – or the next day – as well as today! I'm done here!"

Williams and James looked at each other, puzzled.

Detective Williams was the first to speak. "You're free to go," he said with an air of resignation.

Gambuchi called his service and, in twenty minutes his driver arrived. The ride to his brownstone was quiet; he mopped his face with his handkerchief which was already saturated.

As the car drove off and Gambuchi climbed the steps to his front door he heard his name.

"Gambuchi!"

When he turned the first bullet hit him in the shoulder spinning him around and to the stairs. The man approached.

"Mr. Futcelli sends his regards."

One bullet entered his chest another to his forehead. Gambuchi would not talk.

22

Ben recovered from his injuries and was released from the hospital; the coroner released the body of Margaret Lightstar to Benjamin.

The two of them sat quietly – mostly – throughout the first leg of the trip from Long Island through New York City and Pennsylvania. North of Baltimore, Ben spoke.

"Dad, I don't understand. What happened to mom? I miss her. It hurts, dad."

"Ben, all I know is some bad men came into our house thinking someone else was there, someone they wanted to hurt. And your mom was killed."

"Can you catch them, dad? Can you punish them?"

"Well, that's not really my job, Ben. The police are working hard to find out who did this and punish them. I miss her, too, Ben. Very much."

"Is she...dad, is mom in heaven?"

"Yes, son, she's in heaven. Do you remember the stories she shared with you from the time you were so little? Stories about Jesus? How he was killed – unjustly – and how he died for our sins? Your mother believed that, believed in Jesus. I know she's in heaven, Ben. For sure."

The ride the rest of the way to Annapolis was quiet and Ben dozed off.

When they arrived in Annapolis, Margaret's parents were there to meet them.

Margaret's father, Joseph Karmen was tall and well built. At nearly sixty-five years of age he was still athletic. Forty years earlier, he was captain of the Naval Academy football team, then served in Viet Nam. He is a decorated Navy veteran.

Margaret Johnson-Karmen was born to Baltimore's wealthy elite. Taught at elite private schools, she met and married Joseph Karmen in 1966 and raise one daughter, Margaret. With the loss of her only daughter, Mrs. Johnson-Karmen was inconsolable. From the time of young Margaret's murder, she was in the care of a physician and a psychiatrist for treatment of depression. On this day, she ventured out of her home to greet her son-in-law and grandson.

The body was taken to the mortuary, having been embalmed in New York.

The morning service was lavish. The homily cited Revelation 21:4, "He will wipe every tear from their eyes. There will be no more death or mourning or crying or pain..." When the body was interred, Margaret's mother collapsed and was helped to the limousine. At the Karmen home guests were served refreshments and all offered their condolences. Joseph Karmen took Benjamin aside.

"What happened, Benjamin? Do the police know who did this?"

"The police have their ideas, but can't prove it – yet. It seems it was a mob hit, a case of mistaken identity."

"Son, I still have connections in Naval Intelligence. I can get some unofficial help. Folks I know are quite resourceful."

"No, dad. Let's let the police handle this. I've been told that some people who may have been involved have been killed already: one hit man, a lawyer and a mole in the sheriff's department."

"Call me if you need my help."

"Thanks, dad."

Their embrace was long and clutching.

<23>

As Williams and James turned the corner they were met with a crowd of onlookers. James briefly hit the siren and the crowd separated and a uniform raised the crime scene tape. They parked and got out; they were met by another uniform.

"What do we have, officer?" Detective Williams asked.

"Vic's a white male, late forties, early fifties with three gunshot wounds. ID says he's William Gambuchi. Address on his id says he lives here."

"I want a canvas of the area. Knock on doors. See if anyone saw or heard anything. Did you find any shell casings?"

"No on the casings. I'll get on the canvas right away."

James turned to Williams. "Shooter either was neat and picked up the casings or used a revolver."

"Yeah," Williams said. "We know who was behind this, thing is, how to prove it."

Just then Williams' phone chirped.

"Williams."

Silence.

"Ok. We're on it."

"What's up?" James asked.

"We got another one. Long Island City. Freddy Batamata. Another one of Futcelli's men."

"If we sit back, maybe the case will take care of itself," James retorted.

The pathologist from New York City determined three shots. One to the left shoulder, one to the head and one to the heart. She had no idea, yet, the caliber – likely a .25.

Suffolk County's pathologist examined Freddy's body and found the vic had a broken neck.

Autopsy reports would be forthcoming in both cases.

<24>

"Gather 'round!" Detective Ricardo shouted as he entered the squad room.

As the detective squad gathered in the "war room," Ricardo faced them.

"Why haven't we closed the Lightstar case yet? We got bodies piling up! Futcelli's lawyer was shot last night at his brownstone and one of his mobsters showed up with a broken neck in Long Island City! Whada we got so far?"

The reports were scant. There were no new leads in the case. Mrs. Lightstar was murdered and her son wounded in her home by an assailant or assailants; the hit was ordered – though not proven – by mob boss Toreo Futcelli; the order was delivered by William Gambuchi, mob lawyer; the target was to be an undercover officer, Clete Decker, using the alias Jimmy Vasco; and Amanda Vicardo, SCSD clerk, informed Gambuchi of the UC's identity and address. The Vicardo woman was killed in a car crash; Gambuchi was murdered on his stoop and Batamata's neck was wrung.

"Can you give me anything – anything – that can be of help?"

"Uh, Detective. I think I have something that might help."

"Jimmy, gimme what ya got."

"Well, sir, I checked Amanda Vicardo's phone records from her work station…"

"And?"

"Well, sir, she made one call before, and one call after, her call to the attorney."

"Gambuchi?"

"Yeah, him."

"Well…?"

"Uh, sir, the first call was to The Red Garter and the second call was to Riker's Island."

"Wait. What? Riker's Island?"

"Yes sir, Riker's Island."

"Why? Why call Riker's Island?"

"I don't know sir. I'm not a detective; I'm just a computer guy."

"Get out of here."

"Ok, people, tell me why Ms. Vicardo called The Red Garter, knowing that Gambuchi would be contacting them."

"She didn't know that Gambuchi would make contact?" one sergeant suggested.

"She did know and was making sure the message got to Futcelli's people?" another proffered.

Ricardo suggested something different.

"This was done at the order of Futcelli's people; she didn't know who Gambuchi would contact. An insurance policy because Futcelli don't trust Gambuchi. I want you to work this from every angle. Also, find out who she talked to at Riker's. I have a meeting in five minutes with detectives from Midtown North."

25

Detective Ricardo met with Williams and James in a conference room off the detective's squad room. The case required coordination because the strings were spread out between jurisdictions and needed to be gathered together to form a narrative.

"I'm Detective Williams, this is Sergeant James. Detective Ricardo, this case is getting muddied by the day. Your people worked the case of Amanda Vicardo, accidentally killed in a car crash…"

"Well, that's not exactly accurate. Eye witnesses say she was traveling at a high rate of speed and being pursued by another car, an unidentified black sedan. She lost control on 27A and crashed. The lab says the gas tank ruptured and it was ignited by a lit cigar. Witnesses say the sedan stopped at the accident and threw something from the passenger side window. Probably the cigar. We have made the connection that she was working for Toreo Futcelli as an inside informant, a mole. We can't prove the connection since the only one who can tell us is now dead."

Detective Williams interjected, "Ok. So now we have Gambuchi, Futcelli's lawyer gunned down on the stoop of his brownstone. We had just finished a sit down with him. We know – but like the Vicardo woman, can't prove – that Gambuchi talked with Futcelli's people, who carried out the hit…"

"And we put a lot of heat on him, too. Gambuchi was dripping sweat; I thought he'd talk, but in the end, he refused," James said. "Then he calls his service and gets offed as he walks to his place."

"And we find a DB in an alley, one of Futcelli's hit men. Got his neck wrung," Ricardo said. "Here's what we know so far: Clete Decker, one of yours, was working undercover out of the house in Babylon; he used the alias Jimmy Vasco. Toreo Futcelli was the target and was arrested by a task force of SCSD, NYPD and the FBI. Futcelli orders a hit on Vasco, Vicardo scours SCSD records and passes on information to Gambuchi that Vasco is Clete Decker, Gambuchi schlepps to the Red Garter with a note and the hit is done. Thing is, Vasco/Decker no longer lives at the house in Babylon; the county sold the property to the Lightstar family and the wife gets offed."

"So Gambuchi gets hit by Futcelli's crew, Vicardo gets killed by Futcelli's people...," James stated

"But who killed the hit man?" Ricardo asked.

"Who?"

"I don't know," Ricardo stated. "The only one in this case is your people and our people."

"What's this Lightstar guy? What's he do?"

"Works for a company..." looks through his notes, "...Security International, Incorporated. They provide high dollar security – around the world. He was working a security detail for a UN muckety-muck in the city. I confirmed that through multiple sources. He was sitting on their client until 6 AM and didn't arrive home until about 7:30 when he called 911. We confirmed his whereabouts from his GPS on his car."

Williams asked, "Are these people, SII, capable of this hit, the killing of the hit man?"

"From what I have learned, they are ex-military, ex-spooks. I imagine they would have the means. We have no evidence – none – that they were involved."

"Not only would they have the means, they'd have the motive – family of one of their own was murdered. Let's get a warrant for records on these people," James ordered.

"Sure thing," Ricardo said, "*Judge, I would like you to issue a blanket warrant on a company and its employees, based in New York City. Oh, and I have absolutely no probable cause for said warrant. Would that be ok, judge? Please? Moreover, one of the employees of said company had his wife murdered in this same said case we're pursuing.*"

Detective Ricardo continued, "By the way, it has come to my attention that Amanda Vicardo called the Red Garter just before calling Gambuchi; also, after the call to Gambuchi, she called Ricker's Island. We have not been able to determine why she called the strip club when she had passed information to the lawyer and we don't know who she spoke with at Ricker's."

"With whom," James said.

Ricardo and Williams glared at James.

26

The door to Toreo Futcelli's cell opened and two men entered. The tall one was dressed in a plain gray suit and tie, no pocket handkerchief and carried a briefcase; the second wore a dark blue suit, tie and a handkerchief that was hastily stuffed in the suit pocket. He, too, carried a briefcase.

"What the..." Futcelli started to say as he arose.

"Sit down, Mr. Futcelli. We're here to share information. I'm Robert Swanson, U.S. Attorney for the Southern District of New York and this is Manhattan ADA, Tony Anthony."

Anthony interjected, "We're here to inform you of two circumstances, one bad, and the other very bad. The bad one is that your lawyer, William Gambuchi, Esquire, is dead. He was gunned down on the stoop to his brownstone by a person or persons unknown. We will unravel that, and if it lead back to you and plays out the way we believe it did, you will be charged in his death and our recommendation will be the death penalty."

"Wait! Wait a minute! You can't come bustin' in here like this! I want a lawyer!"

"Well, Mr. Futcelli, it seems you have no lawyer," Robert Swanson replied. "However if you cannot afford one, one will be provided..."

"That's nuts! I can afford an attorney. I can buy attorneys wholesale. I can buy and sell the both of you, for that matter!"

Swanson continued, "The really bad news is the undercover cop, the one you tried to kill, is alive and well. He's eager to testify for the prosecution and he has video and audio recordings of your activities over the last two years. That case is so easy, I could have a clerk try the case. Speaking of clerk, there's the matter of Amanda Vicardo..."

"That's nuts! I didn't kill anyone! And I don't know who this Amanda – something or other – is! I'm an honest businessman and this is a frame. It's all a frame!"

"Just like Al Capone was an honest businessman who got framed for not paying his taxes. An honest citizen," Swanson said.

"Yeah! Just like that!"

"Anyway," Anthony stated, "detectives are piecing everything together. Tell me how this rings: You get busted as the result of an undercover sting, you order the killing of the cop, Amanda Vicardo digs through police records and passes the name and address to Gambuchi, Gambuchi pays a visit to the Red Garter giving the info to your people who do the hit – only it's the wrong people living there now. Gambuchi's dead; Vicardo's dead and one of your hit men is dead.

"Toreo Futcelli," he said as he stepped forward to face him and lean in close, "the net is closing. If we pin any of these killings to you, you get the needle. I'll be there to watch. I will enjoy it."

Swanson stepped in, "However, if you can help us with bigger fish than you, we can see that you are spared the needle. We don't need an answer right away; you can think about it; it's not like you're going anywhere anytime soon. Here's the deal, though: there will come a time when the deal will be off the table. When we unravel this Babylon job, we will have no need of your help."

"Get out of here! Get out! Jailer!" he said as he pounded on the door.

With that, U.S. Attorney Swanson and ADA Anthony left.

But Futcelli was shaken. How could this get bungled like this? And he was enraged. Futcelli turned his mattress over onto the floor and threw his books.

<27>

"But dad. I want to be with you," Ben pleaded.

"I know, son. I have some things to do in New York, then I will come and get you. We will never be apart after that."

"I like gramps and nanna, all right, dad; I just feel so alone. I miss mom so much."

"Mom will always be with you, here," Benjamin said pressing a finger to his son's chest, "in your heart. I love her too and miss her."

"Dad?"

"Yes?"

"Please hurry back to me. I feel so alone now."

"I promise," he said, embracing his son.

Benjamin Lightstar left the small cottage in Annapolis and drove the John Hanson Highway to the I-97 on ramp. Past Baltimore, Newark, Philadelphia, Trenton and through New York City his thoughts were on Margaret, how he missed her, how his hopes and dreams were forever altered.

How could this happen? He had been so consumed with the care of Ben that he was not aware of the progress that had been made in the investigation – by the SCSD, NYPD, and FBI or by SII. Benjamin was not focused on exacting revenge; he wanted, what, justice? Sometimes that concept was little more than smoke, lacking anything substantive. The more he thought about it, the more he merely wanted to know who and why. Through everything, too, he had not had the time for his own grieving.

Using his security badge, he pulled into the parking garage of SII, a steel and glass building four stories tall. The impeccably landscaped lawn with ivy and willows had the appearance of a small town college campus. The elevator opened at the first floor and immediately it was filled. Everyone exited before he reached the fourth floor.

He walked the empty hallway to Bill Sturgeon's office, entered and sat heavily in the chair opposite his boss's desk.

He looked as if he had pushed a boulder up a hill, only to have it roll to the bottom; he was tired.

Bill looked and him for a moment and said nothing. Then he spoke.

"We have a plan."

28

Each day "Jaws" traveled from Port Jefferson on the north shore of Long Island to Bridgeport, Connecticut. Bridgeport & Port Jefferson Steamboat Company operates the service across Long Island Sound.

And Futcelli's people travel as well. Nicki "Lil" Boots runs one of his rings that works the north shore. Her girls work both sides of the sound and generate revenue for Futcelli, lots of revenue. Drugs you sell once; these girls could be sold over and over again.

Kim Soto is one of her girls. Coming to America from Korea, Kim had hoped one day to be on Broadway; petite with shiny black hair, she loved to dance and act. From the time she was barely able to walk she would twirl and sing. It was her dream to sing and dance. When she came to these shores as a late teen, she was met by one of Futcelli's 'agents' who promised her the stars. Her next twelve months were spent in isolation. She was fed regularly but kept apart from everyone. Now she was a prostitute. "Lil" Boots told her that she had to pay for the care that had been given her. Also, she had seen firsthand the punishment that could be exacted upon other girls she met, girls reluctant to fulfill their obligations or who tried to flee.

Wendy Owens came from southern Illinois. She had been reared on a farm by parents who were right out of a Norman Rockwell painting. Or maybe Grant

Wood. These were salt of the earth folks who never missed a Sunday church service. Wendy's passion was fashion. She loved dressing up in the nicest clothes and often went to town to try on the newest fashions; the clerks thought her beautiful. And she was. When Wendy went to New York her folks never heard from her. It had been fourteen months now and they fretted about her.

Cindy Baker was a Californian. She had tried acting and worked some small plays in Fresno. Unable to break through in Hollywood, she struck out for New York. She was young and athletic, a surfer. And beautiful. Her sun bleached hair was long and radiant. Always, she was afraid her time would pass, that she would awaken one day and her good looks would be gone. Dreams die hard and she didn't want to live her life without taking a shot at the brass ring.

Elizabeth Cotton was refined. Having grown up in Connecticut to a wealthy couple she had everything. Sort of. Her parents had worked every day since college – Harvard sweethearts – and didn't stop. A brief pause, long enough to give birth, was the sole interruption to their busy lives. And Elizabeth was shuffled from care giver to care giver. She wanted the love of her parents. They just didn't have the time. No, it wasn't that. They didn't 'make' the time. When Elizabeth was nineteen she rejected her parents' offer of tuition at Harvard and instead was given a trust that provided for her forever.

She took the ferry to Port Jeff and was never seen again. Her tall, graceful figure made her desirable. And profitable.

Camille Jackson was slender and tall with ebony skin and almond shaped eyes. She was truly stunning. Having lived her formative years in rural Georgia, Cami had an urge to be free, to wander and seek adventure. When she first arrived in New York City she was star struck; the bright lights of Broadway were mesmerizing. This was what she wanted. This was what she was born to. Maybe, just maybe her name would be another of those names attributed to stardom, a single name everyone would know. Cami.

As the girls were waiting for the ferry to dock the Suffolk County Sheriff swept in and the girls fled. It was entertaining to watch the women in their short skirts and high heels fleeing the pier and hiding in the shops. The only girl that was the target of this sweep was "Lil" Boots. She was the one farthest up the Futcelli food chain and that was their ultimate objective.

She was cornered in the walkway between the shops on the harbor, one officer in front of her and another behind here. She turned one way, then the other, then looked to the doorways of the shops.

"Boots, stop! Where do you think you can run with those shoes on that we can't catch you?" The officer facing her scowled at her.

She looked down at her feet, then at the cops, then relaxed. She was trapped.

"What do you want with me? I'm just doing some shopping. You can't hassle me!"

"We just want to have a talk with you. Our commander asked us to give you a ride to the station."

"I'm not going with you! Off you!"

"Well," said the one behind her, "we weren't told to *ask* you if you wanted to go, we were sorta *told* to bring you. The car's over here."

The black Suburban observed. It had been in the parking lot thirty minutes ahead of the police.

When they met in the interrogation room, she sat impatiently, strumming her very long fingernails on the desk.

"Look, we know you're one of Futcelli's girls; we know about the prostitutes," Detective Ricardo said, mildly.

"I want my lawyer! I'm not saying anything until Gambuchi shows up," Nicki said.

Pedro and his sergeant exchanged glances.

"You don't know?" the detective asked?

"Know what?" Nicki asked with a disdainful look.

The sergeant opened a manila folder that was by his elbow and slid a crime scene photo across the table.

"Gambuchi's dead," he said. "Shot three times."

Ricardo interjected, "These people don't play nice. If you cooperate we can help you."

"Do you want a court appointed attorney, Nicki?" asked the sergeant.

"No," she fired back, "I want to go. If I'm not under arrest, I'm leaving."

The two looked at each other and shrugged.

"Gambuchi was shot and killed after a sit down with NYPD. He gave up a chance for help and look what happened to *him*," the sergeant said.

"I'll have an officer take you back to Port Jeff harbor," Pedro said.

She was taken back to the pier at Port Jefferson and dropped off.

She paced the sidewalk in front of the pier. Soon the girls returned. Some of them.

"Where's Wendy? And Cami?"

"I don't know, "Lil" Boots. We lost track of 'em after the cops took you," Elizabeth replied. "They were talking to some guy in the parking lot last time I saw them."

"Well at least they were making me some money. Did you?"

"No. But they were just talking. I don't think it was a john."

"Who was it then?"

"We don't know," Cindy said.

"Well, scatter out and look for them! Meet back her in thirty minutes."

The girls would not find Wendy and Cami.

29

Detective Pedro Ricardo studied the Lightstar crime photographs. The pictures of the bedroom and hallway were ones he'd looked at before and he quickly set them to the side. Then he focused on the scenes of the patio entranceway. No prints had been found. Outside – the images looking in from the patio caught his attention. Of particular note were fresh scratches on the wooden deck. He called one of his detectives to confirm what he was seeing.

"Look! Right there on the deck. Do you see the scratches?"

"Yeah, boss. I remember seeing those when the technicians dusted the area; I didn't know what to make of it."

"Did anyone take any measurements of the spacing?"

"Hang on. Let me check my files."

The detective left to retrieve a folder from his desk, then returned.

"Yes...wait, here it is. The spacing of those scratches is twenty four inches."

Detective Ricardo leaned back in his chair. He closed his eyes.

"Did anyone look…up? What is outside on that wall above where the scratches were found?"

The detective spread out the photographs taken of the patio area. Detective Ricardo moved them around, the retrieved one.

"Here! Look at that box on the outside wall. That's an alarm panel. Was there a ladder anywhere nearby?"

"Yes. There was one next to the greenhouse. Probably a ten footer."

"I want you to take one of our lab techs over there and dust the ladder for prints. Check for fibers too. These guys left no other trace; I hope they were sloppy with the ladder."

"What d'ya think, boss? They used the ladder to override the alarm panel?"

"Yeah. I think so. Maybe. Measure the spacing of the legs on that ladder, too."

<30>

Benjamin had a conversation with Detective Ricardo and was frustrated by what he heard, how the investigative team had a "gut" instinct that Toreo Futcelli was behind the slaughter of his wife but that nothing was found to link him to the crime.

The dead bodies piling up around the Futcelli connection was interesting but circumstantial; nothing could prove Futcelli had ordered the hit. And his alibi was solid: he was on Riker's Island.

Bill Sturgeon assembled a team. Clarence Thomas, Agent Reynolds and Benjamin Lightstar. What was known was shared and each member was assigned an area of responsibility. Clarence would scour internet resources for anything that could prove – truly and forensically *prove* – that Futcelli was responsible. Agent Reynolds was assigned the responsibility of talking to the people at the Red Garter, with a not so polite request to practice restraint in his dealings there. Benjamin was tasked with being point person in contacting SCSD, NYPD and the FBI. Benjamin would put a face to the crime in Babylon, one that could not be dismissed or "blown off."

Benjamin took one of the agency vehicles and drove out to Riverhead, Long Island. As he was to learn it was actually, physically located in Riverside. The blue sky was a contrast to the gray sentiment he felt. The chilled air matched his feelings perfectly. The snowy landscape reflected a blue hue to the banks of the Peconic River. The GPS application on his phone led him to the complex and he pulled into a parking space marked "Visitor Parking." Walking inside he found a duty officer at the front desk.

"How can I help you?" he asked. His name tag said he was Joseph.

"Joseph, I'm here to see Detective Ricardo. It's about the murder in Babylon. I'm the husband of the woman who was murdered."

"Hold on while I check. What is your name, sir?"

"I'm Benjamin Lightstar."

"Yes sir. I have a Benjamin Lightstar at the front desk. It's about the Babylon homicide."

Benjamin waited, then the duty officer hung up the phone and looked at Benjamin.

"He'll be right here and escort you back to his office."

"Thanks," Benjamin replied.

Soon Benjamin was in the detective's office and was to learn that no progress had been made. Then he showed Benjamin the photograph of the patio deck and the scratches.

"I don't remember those. When the alarm system was installed, the technicians were very careful. They laid tarps on the deck so they wouldn't scratch the deck. No. They couldn't have been there before that morning."

"There was a ladder next to the greenhouse," Ricardo said. "We think the guys who did this used it to access the alarm system. I have sent a lab guy to check it for any evidence that was left behind."

Benjamin stared for a moment.

"What do you have on Toreo Futcelli? Have you been able to make a connection to this?"

"None we can prove. Yet. The way it's going, we'll need a seriously fortunate break. He will go down on the racketeering charge, that's for sure. The cop, the undercover cop, is ready to testify. Oh, and we're putting some pressure on his operation. We brought in one of his pimps and talked with her. She was pretty shaken when we showed her the crime scene photo of Gambuchi."

"How did that happen? Gambuchi's murder?" Benjamin asked.

"A couple of NYPD detectives out of Manhattan pulled him in for questioning. They tried to get him to roll on Futcelli – almost did, too. Then he clams up and they had to let him walk. No sooner did he get out of his car at his brownstone that he gets killed. There was a guy tailing him when the detectives grabbed him. Mickey Zeno. Some of Futcelli's people alibied him and we couldn't prove otherwise."

"Gambuchi's dead. The Vicardo woman's dead. And one of Futcelli's hit men is dead. Who is left who can prove Futcelli killed my wife?

"We're running down leads on that. There are others in his organization. Maybe they had direct evidence that we can use to nail him.

"You have my number. Call me if I can help in any way. I laid Margaret to rest and young Ben is staying with Margaret's folks in Annapolis."

"Thank you for coming in, Mr. Lightstar. I will do my best to crack this. I *will* stay in touch. I'll have someone show you to the lobby."

Benjamin sat in the car in the parking lot, closed his eyes and prayed to himself.

Dear God! I am alone and in need of your strength. I know well that there will be justice in eternity for what happened. Help me to find justice this side of eternity. Let not evil prevail!

Benjamin wept.

31

At SII in the city, Clarence picked up his phone and dialed Bill Sturgeon's office.

"Sturgeon."

"Bill, this is Clarence. I have burrowed into Futcelli's operation and have found a pending drug deal that will be taking place tomorrow in Smithtown, at the Given County Park."

"Where are the drugs right now?" Bill asked.

"Actually, they're in the office of The Red Garter in Long Island City."

"What time is the deal going down?"

"Eleven AM. Want me to put something together?"

"No. Let me think about this." Sturgeon hung up, then called his operations chief with a plan.

Later that day one of SII's men made a call from a public phone in Huntington to the Suffolk County Sheriff's Department.

"Sheriff's Department."

The muffled voice spoke in a sure, steady staccato.

"A. Drug. Deal. Will. Happen. Tomorrow. At Given. County. Park. Near. The Waterfall. In Smithtown. Eleven. AM."

And the line went dead.

Paul T. Givens was town supervisor of Smithtown in the 1950's. He had moved to New York from West Virginia after he was transferred there by General Electric. His work in the community was both admired and respected and the park bears his name.

With DEA agents and Suffolk County Sheriff's personnel donning town utility uniforms, the Chrysler 300 pulled into the parking lot. Two men wearing dress slacks, polo shirts and leather jackets emerged from the car. Looking around, one man stood at the back of the vehicle, then opened the trunk and retrieved a small suitcase. They made their way to the bull statue across the street – a different drop location that was originally planned.

Moments later a Range Rover parked and two men got out and walked across the street. The surveillance team began taking photographs. The men from the Range Rover exchanged an attaché case for the small suitcase. One of the men from the Chrysler examined the contents of the attaché while one from the Range Rover looked inside the suitcase. Each closed the respective containers and they proceeded to their cars.

At this, the signal was given and four squad cars converged on the vehicles. The surveillance team raced to the four men with guns drawn and they – the men – stopped, put the cases down and raised their hands.

"Down on the ground! Now!"

Each man was handcuffed and put in squad cars. The containers were secured and the men removed to county for processing.

But a curious thing happened when the suitcase containing the drugs was processed by the lab: fingerprints were found on the suitcase belonging to Neal Shanahan, an Irish mobster from Woodlawn. The Irish and the Italian mobs did not generally work together, so this was peculiar, notwithstanding the rarity of finding *any* prints. Nonetheless, NYPD was informed and detectives were sent to inquire of Mr. Shanahan why his fingerprints were found on a suitcase used in a drug deal in Toreo Futcelli's turf.

"What do I know about anythin' happening in Smithtown?" Shanahan declared. "I run an honest enterprise in Woodlawn. I don't leave the city. And if I did, it wouldn't be to go to Long Island! I want me lawyer!"

"We have your prints on a suitcase containing fifteen kilos of coke!" ADA Tony Anthony said.

"I want my lawyer!" Shanahan yelled.

Just then the door to the interrogation room opened and a lieutenant appeared.

"This is Shawn Murphy, Mr. Shanahan's attorney."

Murphy charged into the room, pointed at Anthony and said, "My client has nothin' to say." Then to Shanahan, "Stop talking."

"His prints were on a suitcase full of coke that was involved in a drug deal in Smithtown."

"My client has nothing to say. It might be he was planning on buying some luggage; maybe that's how the prints got on the suitcase. Where his prints on the drugs?"

"There were no prints on the bags of coke."

"Then my client's free to go," Murphy said.

"Yes, but we can make trouble for your client. The U.S. attorney can add this to other matters to make a RICO case against your client. I don't get it, though. Why get mixed up with Toreo Futcelli? He's on Ricker's Island and will go to jail with what we have on him. Why let him bring trouble on you?"

Shanahan jumped up.

"I don't do business with that Italian!" he spat. "I don't need his kind of trouble!" The words rolled out of his mouth in an Irish brogue.

As they reached the street, Shanahan turned to his lawyer.

"I don't need this. Futcelli will pay for this."

His car arrived. Stepping to the curb, he got in the car, shut the door and the car sped away.

32

Detective Williams, turning to his computer screen, typed in vehicle registration information for Gambuchi's import-export business. The print-out was modest, less than a dozen vehicles. Four were set up for Futcelli, one was for Amanda Vicardo, one was for Nicki Boots, one was for Freddy Batamata, one was for Mickey Zeno, and rest were in various names.

The detective called Sergeant James to verify the last few names on the list.

"James."

"Sergeant, can you check some names for me. I got a printout of vehicles registered to the import-export business that Gambuchi was running. Most of the names make sense but there's three I don't recognize. I need you to go to the addresses listed and see what you can find out."

"Yeah. I can do that. Whadaya think?"

"I don't know. If the Vicardo woman had a vehicle from Gambuchi and she was dirty, maybe these three will help us crack this."

"You got it, detective. Send it over and I'll run 'em down."

"I'll bring it to you and we can go together. I wanna see where this goes."

Williams took the printout to Sergeant James and they left in the detective's vehicle.

The first address was in Levittown east of Queens off the Wantaugh State Parkway on Cooper Lane. It was a two story split-foyer with an attached garage.

"Can I help you?" asked the pert middle-aged housewife.

"I'm Detective Williams and this is Sergeant James. We're with the NYPD." He was in uniform and his badge was prominently displayed on the shirt and Williams produced his shield.

"Yes? What's this about?"

"I'm sorry to bother you. Mrs. Baker? It is Mrs. Craig Baker, isn't it?"

Yes. What's this about?" she repeated.

I'm sorry, ma'am, but we're following up on a vehicle registration matter. It's nothing serious."

"Ok. I hope I can help."

"Do you own a grey Mercedes GLE coupe?"

"My husband owns a Mercedes, but I don't know about the model. It's grey."

"Where is the car, ma'am?"

"It's at work, with him."

"Thank you, ma'am. We won't take up any more of your time. Oh, by the way, where does your husband work?"

"He's a guard. At Rikers."

The detective and sergeant looked at each other. "Thank you ma'am."

They got in the car and looked at the printout.

James was the first to speak. "That's a pretty expensive house. Five hundred grand?"

"Maybe more, possibly three quarters of a mil."

"And the car. That's a luxury car. Upwards of a hundred grand?"

"A lot. Let's take a drive to Rikers and find out how a guard at Rikers can afford this lifestyle."

"Wait. If he's not cooperative, the other guards may circle the wagons and we get nothing."

"What are you suggesting?" Detective Williams was puzzled.

"How about we get the ADA to get us a warrant to look at Mr. Baker's financials?"

Williams pulled out his phone and called Assistant District Attorney Abernathy.

"Detective Williams here. Can you get me a warrant for Craig Baker's financials? He's a guard at

Rikers and has a Mercedes owned by the import-export company controlled by William Gambuchi, the late attorney to the mob. I believe he's involved somehow in the Babylon murder."

A pause of considerable length transpired.

"Yes. Yes, it's Suffolk's case but it has tentacles extending into the City. People involved in the case keep getting' dead and we're running out of options.

Williams glanced at James and rolled his eyes.

"The guy's a guard at Rikers and owns a very expensive house and drives a very expensive car. He doesn't make enough to afford either."

Williams mouthed to James, "*We got it.*"

"Give me a call when you have it."

They drove back to the City. And waited.

<33>

"Baker! Phone. Line one."

Craig Baker clicked off the intercom and pushed the button for line one.

"Baker."

"Baby, I don't know if it's anything important. The police were here asking about the car. I didn't know what to say, but I told them we owned the Benz."

"Don't worry about it. I'll deal with it. It's not a big deal."

He hung up and looked around, thinking. *"There's nothing there. What's the big deal about the car?"* But he was worried. *"They can't tie me to Futcelli. Cash payments, everyone. Untraceable."*

There really was nothing to worry about. The next day the warrant was issued and Detective Williams examined Baker's bank accounts: $600 in the checking account, $3500 in a savings account and an IRA worth $18,000. The forensic accountant vouched that everything was legit.

"There's a small problem." The accountant was tall and lanky, clean shaven.

"How's that?"

"Well, the house has a mortgage balance of $700,000 and the monthly payment is $2800. The guy makes less than sixty grand a year. The only deposits to his accounts are from the Department of Corrections."

"How does he do that? Is he behind on his mortgage payments?"

"Nope. He's current."

"Then the money is coming from somewhere. He's got some income he's not reporting."

"That's how I read it."

Williams called James.

"We gotta bring Craig in. His finances are hinkey."

They waited until his shift was over and pulled him over at Hazen Street and 77th.

"We'd like you to come with us, Mr. Baker."

"What for?"

"We want to ask you some questions. As a fellow officer, you want to help us, don't you?"

"Yeah, but I don't know why you want me."

"It'll make more sense when we get to the precinct house. We can make the request official and go through DOC channels is you want."

"No...uh, ok."

The drive to the precinct was quiet. Once in the interrogation room, Craig Baker tried to be cool, but he was definitely nervous.

"We visited your house yesterday and talked with your wife. Nice lady." Sergeant James wanted to ease into the interrogation.

"Yeah, she told me."

Does she work, Mr. Baker?"

"No she doesn't. Why?"

Detective Williams was more aggressive in his questioning. "Well, see, you have a nice house and a nice car. Very nice. Very expensive. How can you afford those on your salary? You make, what, eighty thousand?"

"Something like that."

"The numbers don't add up. We checked and there's no way you can afford this lifestyle. There's some income somewhere that you're not reporting. Outside income."

"And we think Toreo Futcelli is your money man," said James.

"Who? I don't know anybody by that name."

Williams went on the attack. "We know there's hidden income. We got a warrant to go snooping through your finances and next we're gonna get a warrant to search your place. We'll find the money."

"Help us out and we'll help you. Tell us everything and testify against Futcelli and we'll get you witness protection."

"I talk and I'm dead. You got nothing on me. Too many people have turned up dead for me to want to talk to you."

"You think we won't find your stash at your house?"

"You won't find anything there cuz there's nothing there to find."

They had him in interrogation for three hours then had a squad car take him back to his car.

"He's confident," Williams said.

"Could it be he has another place to hide the money?"

"I think so. The way he said 'There's nothing there to find.' Even if we find the money, I don't think we can get him to roll."

James had a thought. "What if we can find the money and he won't roll. We hold him incommunicado and let it out that he *is* cooperating. Futcelli'll find out. He'll slip up. Or how about this: we get him in front of a grand jury, get his testimony and Futcelli threatens to kill him. Once the threat is made we can get the grand jury testimony in without Baker having to testify."

"We have to find the money first. He was too confident; I don't think the money is at his place. We have to look somewhere else."

"Line two, detective." Williams knew the intercom was necessary; he, however, thought it intrusive.

"Williams. Yeah?" The detective began writing on a legal pad. "Ok. We're on it."

"What's that about?"

"James, the accountant found property in Gambuchi's name. On the north shore near Old Field. Let's go."

"Ok, but what do we do when we get there?"

"We look around and ask questions."

With traffic the trip took an hour and twenty minutes. The place was nice with a swimming pool and abutting the beach. A dock and boat house were situated at the water's edge. There was no evidence that the money was buried on the property, however it might be hidden inside.

"Let's have a visit with Mr. Baker once more."

And they drove to Rikers.

"Mr. Baker, we're here to inform you that we are seeking a search warrant for the beach house and boat house at Old Field. We'll have drug sniffing dogs who will sniff out any trace of anything – including money – that has a scent of drugs. We believe we'll find your prints on the money. That ties you into a murder rap."

"I had nothing to do with the hit at Babylon! You can't tie me to that."

"Craig. You just did."

"I want a lawyer. I ain't sayin' anything more."

"We're at your place of employment and not at the precinct. You aren't under arrest. Once we conclude our search, we'll have an arrest warrant."

Detective Williams and Sergeant James left Rikers Island. Men from the Suffolk County Sheriff's Department were posted at the Old Field property. They waited.

At ten o'clock the Mercedes pulled into the driveway and Craig Baker got out, went to the back door and, with a pry bar, jimmied the door. In the back bedroom he retrieved a box from the closet and…stopped.

In the doorway were two detectives.

"Police. Hold it right there."

Baker was shocked and angry.

"You have no business in here. This is an illegal entry."

"You're wrong. We observed an unknown male subject break into this beach house and we investigated. What's in the box?"

"Nothing. It's my property and this is my place."

"Actually, the property is registered to a victim of a homicide, a man named William Gambuchi, esquire. You're trespassing."

The second detective approached with handcuffs and spun Mr. Baker around.

"You have the right to remain silent..."

Baker told everything he knew. He didn't know much, though. He had been on Futcelli's payroll for the past five years. The money that was in the box was his payoff. He passed messages and contraband to Futcelli and any of his men who were in his cell block, the Otis Bantum unit. He took the call from Ms. Vicardo and passed on the information to Futcelli that the lawyer had the information on the hit.

His statement established that the hit came from Futcelli, but it wasn't direct evidence that Futcelli ordered it. Baker wasn't in the cell when the order was given, only that he received the call from Ms. Vicardo. Baker could only testify about that call.

<34>

"They picked up Craig Baker today." Clarence Thomas threw down a pile of papers on Bill Sturgeon's desk. "He'll roll like a marble kicked across the kitchen floor."

"Who is Craig Baker?" Bill Sturgeon tossed his reading glasses on his desk next to the papers and rubbed the bridge of his nose.

"Craig Baker is a guard at Rikers. He's one of Futcelli's men – passes information and favors between Futcelli and the outside."

"Can he get Futcelli on the Lightstar murder?"

"I doubt it unless he was in the cell when the order was given. So, no. That's no help.

"How do we nail him for that?" Bill Sturgeon was fidgeting, drumming his fingers on the desk.

"Unless he confesses – which is unlikely – we won't be able to prove it. The only one left who can testify that the hit came from Futcelli is the guy in charge of The Red Garter. Agent Reynolds had a, er, conversation with him and got Freddy Batamata's name, the shooter."

"How can we incentivize Futcelli to confess? What would make him prefer going to jail to some alternative?" Sturgeon, eyes narrowed, was thinking out loud.

"We already implicated the Irish mobster, uh, Neal Shanahan, in one of Futcelli's drug deals. He's plenty sore, Shanahan. I suppose we do the same to another mobster, Puerto Rican or Russian. Futcelli still has his prostitution ring working the docks at Port Jefferson; maybe we involve the Albanians."

Sturgeon sat upright and closed his eyes. Opening them he said, "See what you can come up with in that regard; I don't care which bunch we use. I think it's time to put a squeeze on Futcelli.

Thomas went to his office and thought about how to "influence" Futcelli into confessing. The options would narrow absent a confession – narrow to only one.

It's unlikely we can snatch a girl from the Albanians and put her in 'Lil Boot's stable, not unless there's a lot of gun-play. The Russians wouldn't just get angry, they'd get to Futcelli and kill him. Well...that would take care of things, wouldn't it? Maybe we don't care if he confesses; maybe all we care about is he pays for the murder he surely commissioned.

Clarence had created an algorithm to search anything on the name "Futcelli." He tapped a few keys on his computer and found that a plane arriving from Sicily would land at Kennedy tomorrow afternoon. On that flight was one Giaimo Futcelli.

He picked up the phone.

"Reynolds."

"Yeah."

"There's a flight coming into Kennedy from Sicily tomorrow. Put a tail on one of the passengers, Giaimo Futcelli. I need to know where he goes and who he talks to. Stop by my office and I'll have a note with the particulars."

"Sure thing."

It was no surprise that Giaimo's first stop was the Red Garter. Their conversation was picked up by the wire that was planted on Reynolds' previous visit.

"Ramone, I came a long way to fix this mess for my brother. How could you fu..."

"I don't know what happened, Mr. Futcelli. I got the name and address from the girl and I passed it to Freddy. He did the hit but it was the wrong people. It was the right house but the cop wasn't there anymore."

"What's his name?"

"Who?"

"The cop, you idiot!"

"Oh, Decker. Clete Decker."

"Where do I find this Clete Decker?"

"I don't know. If I knew, he'd be dead by now."

"I got a shipment coming in by boat. It'll be here tonight. Get someone to make a delivery tomorrow afternoon at Three Villages in Stony Brook. Two men. You'll meet the buyers at one of the restaurants there, eat lunch and make the exchange."

Like reading an old newspaper, the plan was exactly the same as in Smithtown. Prints of the Puerto Rican mob boss were transferred to the container that was stored at the Red Garter, then the Suffolk County Sheriff's office was notified.

<35>

Benjamin met with the SII's alarm control division at the Babylon house in order to restore the alarm system. They took the usual precautions of laying a tarpaulin on the patio deck before putting up the ladder. The technician opened the panel.

"They used foam to disable it. I brought another panel."

He worked for the next hour removing the panel and pulling the cabling back inside the house.

"We'll install the new panel indoors, in a closet, maybe."

"There's a closet in the hallway by the front door."

Several of the cable weren't long enough to reach the closet and were extended by splicing new cable onto the existing cable. By late afternoon the alarm system was activated and the technicians left.

"*If they had installed this in the closet from the beginning...*" Benjamin sat on a chair at the kitchen table and wept. And prayed. Then he called the number in the 410 area code.

"Karmin residence."

"Tony, this is Ben."

"How are you holding up, son?"

"Not well. This is nothing like anything I've ever experienced."

"I can't imagine what you're going through. Care to talk to young Ben?"

"Yeah. Put him on."

There was a pause, then the boy picked up the phone.

"Dad! Hi. When are you coming to get me?"

"Soon, son. We're making progress on finding the people who did this to you and your mom."

"I still miss her, dad. Every day I think about her. I'm being tough, though."

"Ben, you don't have to be tough. It's ok to be sad and to cry. In everything, though, keep praying for peace. Remember what you were taught: 'Whatsoever you ask in My name, it will be given to you.'"

Ben could hear his son's sobs. There was nothing he could say to comfort his son except, "I love you, son. I will come for you soon.

"I will pray. I will pray that the killer gets what he deserves."

"Pray for a heart like your mother's. Pray for comfort and peace. Pray, not for vengeance, but for justice."

"I will. Thank you for calling. I was missing you, too."

"I love you and miss you, Ben."

Benjamin hung up the phone and sat quietly for a while. He couldn't get out of his mind the warmth, gentleness and love Elizabeth had for him and Ben.

He called Bill Sturgeon.

"Hello, Benjamin. Did the alarm people get your system working again?"

"Yeah. They installed a new panel in the entryway closet. What's going on with the case?"

"We're working on a plan; I can't tell you over the phone. The threads that connect to Toreo Futcelli are being severed one by one; there's not much left to connect him to the shooting. We're working on it though. Get a good night's rest and we'll talk in the morning."

"I'm anxious to get busy and wrap this thing up. See you tomorrow."

It was a restless night. Every sound the house made, every groan and creak had him bolting out of bed. When weariness finally overcame him he slept. His alarm went off at five o'clock and he prepared for his day.

<36>

There was no doubt who the two pair of men were. The leather jackets, wrap-around sunglasses, slicked back black hair and polo shirts were signs that these belonged together.

"I hope you made it all right and that your health is good." The locals had no trouble recognizing their companions from Sicily.

"I'm good."

"You hungry? Ready to eat?"

"Amunninni."

The locals looked perplexed by the Sicilian word.

"It means 'let's go.' So let's go eat."

They were ushered to a table and looked over the menu. The waiter was helpful with his recommendations. "Try the oysters and the scallops. They're fabulous."

"Se."

The waiter understood Italian and the Sicilian word was close enough to 'si.' The waiter brought the oysters and the wine. No one talked about the shipment, for fear they might be overheard.

One of the Sicilians looked around the table, then at the food and proclaimed, "Mancia! Eat!"

None of them hesitated at the invitation to eat. As the Sicilians picked up an oyster, the tattoo on the back of their right hand was visible: the Trinacria.

Giaimo wasn't there; his job was to ensure the death of Clete Decker so that his brother would be freed. And these Sicilians were only there to ensure the transaction was completed and to take a cut – a very large cut – of the proceeds.

With lunch over, one of the Sicilians instructed the locals that the swap was to take place in the parking lot of the Stony Brook Yacht Club. It would be quick, he told them, drugs and the money would be transferred from the trunk of one vehicle to the other.

The Sicilians watched in horror when, the moment the exchange took place, the Suffolk County Sheriff's deputies moved in and arrested the men.

They were booked and the evidence was processed.

On the attaché case that contained the drugs was the right index fingerprint of Mateo Juan Alvarez, the Puerto Rican mob boss from Bensonhurst.

"Futcelli doesn't discriminate, does he? He works with the Irish and the Puerto Ricans. Let's give Mr. Alvarez a visit."

The information was passed to NYPD detective Williams. Williams and James drove to Bensonhurst, pulled up to the restaurant that was a known hangout for Mateo Juan Alvarez. As the detective and the sergeant approached the door, two Puerto Ricans blocked their path.

"You don't want to do that, do you?" James asked as they flashed their badges.

The two men stepped aside without a word.

Approaching Mr. Alvarez's table, they produced a photograph of the attaché case, opened to reveal the drugs and another of Alvarez's fingerprint.

"What's this? Means nothing to me. You cops always trying to get me for something. I'm an honest businessman."

"It should mean a lot to you. Twenty-five years, as a matter of fact."

"What? You come in here and show me these pictures and I'm supposed to be afraid?"

"You should be. The fingerprint is yours. On a case with a lot of drugs. How did you get hooked up with Futcelli?"

"You crazy? I don't do no business with that Italian."

"When we can make a solid case your business with Futcelli will be as cell-mates in Rikers."

"I got nothing to say. If all this was really true and not a set-up, you'd have me in cuffs already and on my way to jail. You got nothing and I got nothing to say."

With that Alvarez turned his back and drank his coffee.

Williams and James looked at each other and walked to the door. Stopping, Williams turned to Alvarez. "We'll make the case all right. Then we're coming back."

When they drove away, Alvarez turned to his companions.

"Futcelli got me mixed up in his business and he gonna pay. I want someone to get to him at Rikers and let him know. Don't have him killed. Yet. Just let him know what's coming. When he won't know it's coming."

The jail-cell communications network passed this information along and when Futcelli's meal was brought to him, he was stunned to see a rat on his plate. He called for the guard, who took his plate away – the only evidence of the intimidation. Later, the guards denied Futcelli's allegations, claiming the prisoner had recently been acting erratically.

"I'm not crazy! It was a rat. A dead rat. The guards looked at each other with confused looks, then denied the prisoner's claims.

"Warden, this is not true. I brought him his food, he ate it and I took his tray away. There was no rat."

"There was, I tell you!"

As the warden and the guards walked away, one guard looked back, glared and raised a clenched fist at Futcelli.

For the first time, Futcelli was genuinely scared. Terrified. Even behind locked doors he didn't feel safe.

He sat on his bunk in a ball.

Over the course of the next two weeks, he was threatened; during his exercise time an inmate would flash a shiv or an inmate would make a slashing gesture across their throat. By the end of the two weeks, he would enter the exercise area and collapse in a fetal position by the door until it was time to return to his cell.

Then Williams and James paid him a visit.

"Hey, what happened to you? You look like hell." Williams was stunned by the change in Futcelli's appearance. He had lost weight and his hair was falling out.

"They're gonna kill me!"

"Who's going to kill you, Toreo?

"Everyone! They're all trying to kill me!" Futcelli was so agitated that Williams and James looked at each other with genuine concern. He was good for the Lightstar murder and Decker could put him away on the drug and prostitution charges, but they didn't want him to be shanked before they could get him on these charges.

"What do you want from us? Pretty soon you're going away for the original charges; you won't avoid that. I can talk to the feds and perhaps I can get the U.S. attorney to make some arrangements whereby you serve your time somewhere nobody will get to you. How does that sound?"

<37>

Toreo Futcelli pled guilty to the original charges. He pled *nolo contendere* to the homicide of Elizabeth Lightstar. The charge was that he was attempting to kill a witness in the original matter, thus making it a federal charge. Benjamin Lightstar was at the sentencing and testified to the impact the murder of his wife had on him and his son, Ben.

Toreo Futcelli was handed down a sentence of twenty-five years for the original charges and life without parole on the murder charge.

Detective First Class Pedro Ricardo was inconsolable, in that the murder had taken place in his jurisdiction and Suffolk County couldn't charge Futcelli in the case. All their hard work for nothing and he let U. S. Attorney Swanson know it. Interagency cooperation might be harmed, he said.

Nicki 'Lil Boots ended up with the entire Port Jefferson operation, that is, the operation sans a couple of her girls.

Abernathy wasn't happy either. The Manhattan prosecutor wanted a piece of Futcelli but was left grabbing at air.

The only people who were happy were the feds. Swanson got his win. That was it. Elizabeth was still dead. That was the harshest reality.

It was never understood which faction scared Futcelli into his confession. Was it Shanahan's people? Was it Alvarez's people? The thought that either of them would merely intimidate him and not just kill him was perplexing. Yet it was better this way, if 'better' can be used to describe anything about this. At least this way it was official that Futcelli was behind the murder of Benjamin's wife.

The following weekend a car pulled into the driveway of the Babylon house. Three people exited the car.

"Welcome home, Ben," said Benjamin Lightstar as he embraced his son. "Welcome home."

The Case of the Bird Who Knew Too Much

A burglary at a Trenton, New Jersey apartment leads to a no-so-routine investigation involving a decades-old federal crime. The only witness to the crime is dead – a parrot.

<>

Helen McGintus, 39, of Trenton, New Jersey, got off work at 5:05 PM on the afternoon of September 9, 2002 and went to her apartment. When she got off the elevator she noticed her apartment door was open. Upon entering she noticed the apartment was in disarray; things were scattered about the floor and overturned. To her horror she found her parrot dead, on the floor of its cage. She called the police.

The police arrived. A uniform policeman was stationed at the door and two uniforms were ordered to canvas the floor for anyone who saw or heard anything. Two detectives, a photographer and a fingerprint technician went over the apartment. The parrot was placed in a paper bag and sealed; a label was attached with the case number on it.

"I'm Detective Roberts and this is Detective Cody. Is anything missing, Miss McGintus?" The lead detective was in his forties and wore a dark suit and a black tie. He was six feet tall and lean. His partner was shorter and rotund, dressed in a grey suit and a red tie.

"Well, yes. My camera bag is missing. I keep it in my bedroom closet. That's all that's missing. I have some jewelry in a wooden box on my dresser, but none of it was taken. The camera, lenses and filters are worth about $500. The jewelry is worth about two thousand dollars."

"I notice some electronics. None of it is taken. The television, the stereo." Detective Cody had been with the photographer, giving instructions and had just entered the conversation.

"No. Only the camera." Helen McGintus dabbed at her cheeks occasionally. "Lolita was my dearest companion," she lamented.

"Lolita?" Detective Roberts and Detective Cody looked at Miss McGintus and then at each other. They were quite puzzled.

"Oh, I'm sorry. Lolita was my parrot. She is, was, an Amazon Parrot. She was intelligent and chatty, requiring lots of attention. She may have made a squawk when the apartment was broken into; maybe that's why she was killed. She can be very noisy."

"What can you tell us about the camera?" Roberts was taking notes as they questioned her.

"It was an entry level digital camera. I bought it almost ten years ago. Once I learned some of the elements of photography I mostly used a medium format, film camera that I would rent. I can't afford to buy an expensive professional camera like that. In fact I had just been out last weekend taking some pictures around town. I returned the equipment on my way to work this morning. They will have the film developed by Wednesday."

"Did you notice anything unusual when you were taking pictures this weekend? Anybody upset that they were photographed?" Detective Roberts stood more erect and was interested in this aspect of the case.

"No. Not that I noticed."

Detective Roberts handed her his business card as the maintenance supervisor came to repair the door. The door wasn't damaged, though; the lock had been picked. The super left after craning his neck to see what had happened.

"Call us if you think of anything that can help us. I'm of the opinion this is more than a simple burglary. Thank you."

She stood, looking at the card as they left.

In the car, Roberts and Cody discussed the case.

"No. This is more than it appears. I think she took one too many pictures this weekend and whoever she shot wanted the pictures destroyed."

"And when they examine the digital camera, they won't find the picture or pictures they're after. They may come back. Miss McGintus could be in trouble."

"Let's find them before they come back."

From the apartment building they went to the pathologist's office.

"Hello gentlemen. To what do I owe the honor?" Dr. Sharon Houston was a young thirty-ish woman with wire framed glasses that sat low on her nose, making her look older than she was.

Cody placed the evidence bag on the stainless steel table.

"Can you give us the cause of death?" Roberts noticed the puzzled look on Dr. Houston's face.

"They don't usually come here in a paper bag. What's up?"

"Well, this is not your usual vic."

She opened the bag, looked inside, then looked at the detectives.

"A macaw?"

"A female Amazon Parrot. Lolita."

"You want me to tell you how it – she – died?"

"She was a witness to a burglary," Cody said, deadpan.

"Well, she ain't talkin'." Dr. Houston's sense of humor was dry, perhaps as the effect of her line of work.

"Can you give us cause of death?" Roberts asked, giving her a wry look.

"Probably."

"Thanks."

Leaving the pathologist's office they went to the camera store and confirmed the facts as Miss McGintus had told them. She had rented a Contax 645 medium format SLR camera, a 140mm lense, an 80mm lense, eight rolls of Ektar 100 film, and twelve rolls of Porta 400 film.

"What's that, about 24 pictures on a roll?" Detective Roberts was considering the labor required to take that many pictures.

The lady behind the counter was young and about college aged; attractive. "On 35mm that would be true. There are eight exposures on a roll of medium format film. Miss McGintus was an avid photographer. She would go out about once a month and bring back several rolls of film. She's good; almost at a professional level. She could be a pro if she did it full time."

"So there's, what, twenty rolls would be 160 pictures." Roberts gave the lady his card. "Call me when they're done."

"Yes sir."

They left the camera shop and headed to the precinct to see what the fingerprint people had, which was nothing.

"The only prints in the place belonged to the lady. She must not have had guests. That's unusual, but not unheard of."

Just then the phone rang.

"Roberts. Uh-huh. What? Really. Ok."

Roberts put the phone down and turned to Cody. "The bird got its neck wrung."

"No surprise there," Detective Cody replied. "Probably made a lot of noise."

"What is a surprise is that Lolita is a boy bird."

"How did Dr. Houston figure that out?" Cody looked surprised.

"I suppose she looked for girl bird body parts and found boy bird body parts. How would I know? She is a doctor; doctors know these things. Let's have a look at the crime scene photographs? Do we have those yet?"

"No. I'll call and find out what's the holdup."

Cody picked up the phone to call the photo lab, but before the call was answered the technician came through the door with the pictures.

"Here's the pictures." The older, balding man dropped the stack of photographs on Roberts' desk and left. Each picture was examined but nothing was found of any help.

"I looked the scene over and didn't see any blood or fibers, nothing the perp left behind. Hopefully there will be something taken from the scene that can tie the doer to the scene." Cody was disappointed at the lack of any evidence at the scene. "Whoever broke into Miss McGintus' apartment knew how to not leave prints or evidence."

On Wednesday morning, Detective Roberts' phone rang. The call was less than a minute. "We'll be right there." Getting up he looked around the room. "Cody! Let's go."

Together they left the precinct.

"What's up?"

"The photographs are ready."

After a discussion concerning payment for services rendered and a reply that the camera store could file for a voucher, Roberts gave the store the case number and they left the store.

The room was clean with several computers and machines used to process sound and video source material. This was the forensics A/V processing center.

"Detectives. What's up?" Duane Breslen was twenty-four and a graduate of Rutgers. He had completed instructions at Quantico in processing sound and video signals.

"I want you to look at some photographs. Can you do facial recognition on these?" In Roberts' hand was a stack of over a hundred photographs.

"That's a lot of pictures. I can do it, but understand that each picture has to be analyzed individually and may take several minutes each. You're talking days or weeks to process all of these." The technician looked through the pictures and began setting some to the side. "There are a number of scenics – no people in them. We don't have to do those. Blauguard Island and Rotary Island. I recognize these of the West Trenton Railroad Bridge. Absent the scenics we're down to about fifty or so photographs. There are some from inside and outside the Cathedral of St. Mary of the Assumption on North Warren Street and at the Patriot's Theater. Here are a handful taken at the State House. I'll call you if I find anything; I know you'll be calling me."

"I hope you find something." Detective Roberts was hopeful. "We need you to rush these."

"By the way, what am I looking for?"

"I wish I knew. Somebody, but I don't know who. Maybe a bad guy. Maybe somebody who doesn't belong."

<>

"There's nothing here. No pictures on the camera."

"Maybe she is having it developed."

"No, Carlos, it's a digital camera. There is no film. Look, I can't let those pictures be found."

The two men dressed casually and nearly identically. It was so because they were brothers. Freddy and Carlos Riati were born in Paterson, NJ to an immigrant family. Freddy became an investment banker. Carlos ran a produce wholesale company. They looked and acted in so closely a manner, it was hard to tell which one was Freddy and which one was Carlos, except that Carlos was half a foot shorter.

In the spring of 1990 the United States Attorney for the District of New Jersey indicted Freddy for investment fraud. They charged that he had swindled investors out of more than $100 million. Simply put, Freddy was running a Ponzi scheme. Early investors received returns generated from investments by later investors. Freddy received the bulk of the investments. Forensic accountants had ample evidence for a conviction.

That summer a small water craft owned by Freddy exploded at the Hudson River inlet near Staten Island. The body was obliterated with no means of identification. One femur was found floating in the water that a forensic anthropologist identified as belonging to a man of Freddy's stature. The clothes fragments, what remained, were consistent with Freddy's wardrobe and the identification – a passport – that was found floating in the water was that of Freddy.

Investigators were suspicious. The family insisted that Freddy be listed as dead and that his case be closed. Officially, it was; unofficially investigators were suspicious. Freddy's death became a cold case.

"If papa hadn't a died, I wouldn't be in Trenton at the church. It's bad enough I couldn't see my father in the coffin or comfort momma, some broad is taking pictures at the church and I know she got me with her camera. If that gets out, I go to prison."

"She wouldn't know you from Romulus or Remus. What's she gonna do? Hand them over to the police? Fat chance, Freddy."

Freddy sat heavily on the edge of the motel's bed. He wondered if he was being overly cautious. Carlos could be right – the woman wouldn't do anything with the pictures. Unless. Freddy wondered if his fear – was it paranoia – might have backfired on him. If the lady called the cops, they would investigate and wonder why the only thing taken was the camera.

"We should have grabbed the jewelry and some electronics – something."

"Why, Freddy? All we wanted was the camera."

"That's the point. Carlos, if she called the cops, they're gonna want to know why the camera was the only thing taken. So, maybe, they ask her where she was. Maybe they look through the pictures. Maybe we just brought trouble on ourselves by going after the girl."

"Then you gotta leave."

"I gotta see ma first."

"But they're watching her."

"She'll go to confession on Friday. Like clockwork, she goes to confession every Friday morning. If I have to sneak in on Thursday and hide out, I will. I can't leave until I see momma."

<>

"He should have been there. I'm sure he was."
Angel Martinez was an FBI Special Agent assigned to
the New Jersey Bureau. He was discussing a detail from
Saturday afternoon with Special Agent Robert Terry.

"Well, perhaps if we had gone inside the
Cathedral of St. Mary of the Assumption we would have
found him." The Requiem Mass for Freddy's father,
Giovani Riati, was that Saturday and the FBI had
stationed agents around the cathedral. They suspected
that if Freddy Riati was truly alive and not the victim of
a tragic boating accident, he would pay his respects to
his father. The agents did not see him. They were
instructed not to enter the church and, so, watched from
places stationed around the church.

"If…"

"Bobby, I know he was there. I can feel it. Even
at the grave site service, I thought we'd catch him. He's
alive as much as you and I."

"You're obsessed."

"I worked the case in '88 and '89. There were a
lot of man hours tracking down victims and a lot of
hours spent by the forensic accountants sorting through
the records. The U.S. Attorney was certain of a
conviction and pledged not to accept a plea deal. Freddy
was going to prison for a long time. Everyone who
worked the case was disappointed when the boat

exploded and many of us smelled a set up. There weren't enough forensics to identify the body. Freddy's passport was the only identifying trait – funny how everything was obliterated except the passport was intact. Officially, the case is closed; unofficially, we keep searching. When the old man croaked, we thought we'd catch him. Another lead that didn't pan out."

"Maybe he *is* dead, Bobby."

"Maybe he's not. If not, we'll find him. Anyway, the boss is pretty sore about our Saturday venture. A lot of time spent for nothing, she's saying. She's only five-six, but don't let her get in your face; she's a pit bull on steroids. With lipstick."

"I'm glad you're the senior agent."

"When the body was placed in the hearse and Mrs. Riati was placed in the limo, I was sure – out of respect for Mr. Riati – Freddy would be there. I was ready to arrest him after the gravesite service. He was a no-show."

"I wasn't happy turning in the 302 on Saturday's events. It was filled with suppositions and little on facts: 'surveillance of suspect at the Cathedral of St. Mary of the Assumption, Saturday, September 7, 2002. Four agents assigned looking for one Freddy Riati at the funeral of his father Giovani Riati. Freddy Riati was presumed to have been killed in a boating accident in 1990, however the body was not positively identified.

The result of the surveillance was negative.' That got me a visit to the boss's office and a chewing out. A year after 9-11, she said, we have better things to do that to chase vapors of the past. Had we caught up with Freddy, we'd be heroes; instead, we're schmucks."

"If he's here, she'll visit his mother. We'll catch him then."

"Yeah, well, we've got orders to stay away. The Bureau isn't going to pay for us to dig into this any further." Special Agent Terry was noticeably upset at having the investigation quashed.

"So we look into this on our own."

"The only shot we'll have is when she goes to confessional on Friday afternoon. If Freddy's in town, he'll be there."

"Done," Angel declared.

<>

The phone rang at Detective Roberts' desk. The detective sprinted across the room and picked up the handset.

"Roberts. On our way."

Detective Cody sat at attention, rose from his chair and followed Detective Roberts. "Where to?"

"The lab. Duane has something for us."

They took the elevator to the third floor, walked the hallway to the Technical Laboratory, and entered. Duane Breslen greeted them.

"I found what you were looking for. Does the name Freddy Riati mean anything to you?"

Roberts and Cody looked at each other, then at Duane.

"No," the echoed.

"He was on two of the photographs from the church. The lady had taken pictures inside the church of the architecture and got Freddy in the frame."

"Ok, so who is this guy?"

"Freddy Riati was indicted by the U.S. Attorney for New Jersey on investment fraud in 1990. In the summer, his boat exploded near Staten Island and the remains were alleged to have been Freddy's; the only thing that identified him was his passport. The body was so scattered there was no way to positively identify the body. The FBI has been looking for him – at least some in the FBI have been looking for him."

The picture was blown up and displayed on a large screen. On the next screen was a police file photograph. Except for the image at the church being an older man, they were the same person.

"Give me a print-out of the two pictures and an enhanced blow up of them."

Duane tapped a few keys on his computer and the printer whirred to life.

"Wait a couple of minutes before you pick them up; the ink has to thoroughly dry."

When the print had dried, Detective Roberts took the photographs and the two detectives returned to their office. Detective Cody, curious, accessed VICAP, the Violent Crime Apprehension Program. Freddy's name did not appear. There was a hit on the N-DEx database, however. It listed information on the warrant against Freddy and listed a contact at the FBI, Robert Terry, and a phone number. A general Google search returned the death and funeral of Giovani Riati that occurred the previous weekend.

Cody took the N-DEx and Google printouts off the printer and shared it with Detective Roberts.

"This is why Helen's apartment was broken into. Freddy Riati faked his own death, but was compelled to visit his father's funeral. Even though he stayed in the background, Helen McGintus inadvertently took his picture when she was inside the church. Thankfully, she wasn't very respectful of the funeral service that was taking place; she just took picture after picture. There's contact information for the FBI. They'll want to see the pictures.

Detective Roberts dialed the number. It rang several times, then was picked up.

"Special Agent Terry, this is Detective Roberts over at Trenton PD. I have some information that will interest you. I have photographs of Freddy Riati at the funeral of his father, Giovani Riati taken last Saturday at the Cathedral of St. Mary of the Assumption."

There was a pause. Detective Roberts twirled his pen in his hand while he listened to the response..

"Ok. I'll see you when you get here. Just ask for Detective Roberts when you get to the front desk."

Thirty minutes later, Special Agents Terry and Martinez appeared, examined the photographs. Special Agent Terry exhaled a deep breath.

"I knew he faked his death; I knew he was alive. If we'd have been allowed inside, we would have got him."

"What now?"

"I believe he will try to see his mother on Friday. She always goes to confession on Fridays. He will want to see her." Agent Terry was nearly giddy at the prospect of nabbing Freddy.

"We have an open burglary case that we believe he is involved in. We can send someone into the church – in disguise."

"We're officially off the case. I got chewed out over our surveillance on Saturday. Nothing to show for our time and my boss was plenty mad."

"Let me put you in my cell phone and I'll call you if we find him. We can have one or two people inside and two or three outside. We'll wait until he's outside before we grab him."

They exchanged numbers and Special Agent Terry left. Roberts contacted his lieutenant to inform him. A task force of five people and the two detectives was set up.

Three people were inside – two female officers and one male; two outside, one near the front entrance and one near the rear entrance. Detectives Roberts and Cody were stationed near a side entrance. Each person had a radio equipped with an earpiece and a small microphone. At different times within a one hour time frame the officers stationed themselves in position. The women were dressed in long robes with head coverings.

They lit candles and kneeled in the front and back pews. The man was dressed in shabby clothes and milled around at the back of the church, occasionally walking to the front to light a candle, then return to the rear. One of the officers stationed outside was dressed in an expensive suit and wore ostentatious jewelry. The other was dressed as a priest, with a collar, and smoking a cigarette.

St. Mary of the Assumption was dedicated in 1871 six years after Anthony Smith purchased the property. It sits on a part of what was once the Battle of Trenton, 1776. It sits at North Warren Street south of Passaic Street. A gymnasium and a convent are located across Passaic; the convent faces North Warren and the gymnasium faces Passaic. Wrought iron fencing surrounds most of the church building and a large gated parking lot is located on the west side of the campus.

Everyone was set up by 9:00 AM Friday morning. It wasn't known when Mrs. Riati would show up. The team members stuck to their assigned rolls. At 11:00 AM Juanita Riati walked through the door, dips her finger in the Holy Water, crosses herself and walks to where the candles are. She lights a candle, kisses the fingers on her right hand and moves slowly to a pew. Sitting, she daps her eyes with a handkerchief, folds her hands and prays.

The officers are watching her with heads bowed. The officer in the rear comes forward, lights a candle and returns to the rear. He has confirmed the identifications and nods to the others as he passes.

"Blessings," he says as he passes his colleagues. This was said as he activated his microphone, the signal that Mrs. Riati was sighted.

The door of the confessional opens and a short, elderly woman exits. Mrs. Riati enters.

For twenty minutes she is in the confessional.

"What could she have to confess for that long?" The officer, not being Catholic nor a woman, didn't know what happens in a confessional.

At 11:30 Mrs. Riati exits the confessional. As she walks to the exit she is approached by a man stooped and supporting his weight with a cane.

"I'm sorry for your loss."

"Thank you. Eh, do I know you?"

"Yes." He paused before whispering. "It's me. Freddy."

The officers were watching. When she embraced him, and collapsed, they knew. It was Freddy Riati. One of the female officers walked to the rear of the church.

"Are you all right?" She took her by the arm and helped her to her feet; the officer didn't look at Freddy.

"Y-yes. I'm fine." Her voice was frail. How soon would it be until she joined her husband, the officer thought?

The officer glanced at Freddy. "God bless you." As the officer said this, she activated her microphone. Everyone on the team knew that there were eyes on Freddy.

Freddy and his mother exited the church and walked down the steps to the sidewalk. As her driver opened the rear door of the car, Detective Cody took Freddy by the arm as Roberts helped Mrs. Riati into the car then closed the door.

Freddy broke away from Cody's grip and took off. The officers from inside the church were now in pursuit of Freddy. The women looked nearly comical holding the long dresses up exposing their running shoes. The male officer wasn't going any faster. Fortunately Freddy wasn't in good shape. He had been living a life of luxury, a sedentary life, and was nearly doubled over from exhaustion. They caught him in front of the Christian Science Ready Room on State Street.

Freddy Riati didn't put up a struggle; he was too tired. Cody had to wait for him to stand up before he cuffed him. A cruiser pulled up and Freddy was placed in the back seat.

Roberts pulled his phone out of his pocket and called Special Agent Robert Terry.

"We got him. He's on his way to booking."

<>

"Freddy, the U.S. Attorney for the District of New Jersey has an open case against you for fraud. You will be charged for the homicide of the man you blew up on your boat. You won't ever see your mother again."

"I'll get bail and…"

"Oh, no! You aren't getting bail. You have a history of flight. Yours is the picture that's in the dictionary under 'flight risk.' I will enjoy seeing you prosecuted for homicide. First degree, too. You killed your victim with intent to flee prosecution. That's first degree. New Jersey still has the death penalty."

There was a knock at the door. The door opened and a woman enters.

"Freddy, don't say anything else." Turning to the detectives she announced, "I'm Freddy Riati's attorney, Jody Frank. I'd like a moment with my client."

Detectives Roberts and Cody left the room. Ten minutes later there's a knock on the glass window.

As the detectives enter, the attorney stands. "As the attorney of record for Mr. Riati, anything he may have said to you from the moment you apprehended my client is inadmissible, inasmuch as I was not informed of his arrest until recently."

"Get up," Roberts ordered Freddy. "You're under arrest for the murder of John Doe. You have the right to remain silent, anything you do say, can and will be used against you in a court of law; you have the right to an attorney, if you cannot afford an attorney, one will be provided for you. Do you understand these rights?"

Freddy nodded.

"Do you understand these right?"

"Yeah, yeah. I understand."

"Can we talk, detectives?" She wasn't intimidated but she was confident.

"Sit down, please." Roberts was curious.

"My client would like to make a deal."

"I can't make a deal on the federal charges. The homicide might be a different matter, except..."

"Except what?"

"The homicide occurred in coastal waters, off of Staten Island. The district attorney will have to decide if it's a Jersey crime, a New York crime, or a Federal crime. Until that's decided, I'm treating it as a New Jersey crime."

"What if it wasn't a homicide?"

"What?" Cody couldn't believe what he was hearing. "The guy was blown up beyond recognition. How could it not be a homicide?"

"If he was already dead."

The detectives looked at each other in bewilderment.

"You can argue that with the DA."

There was a knock at the door. Detective Roberts opened it and a well-dressed muscular man entered.

"I'm Blake Jacoby, U.S. Attorney for the District of New Jersey. I am taking custody of Freddy Riati. Here's the order from U.S. District Court of New Jersey signed by Judge Wagoner." The order was handed to Detective Roberts.

"That didn't take long." Detective Roberts showed no emotion as he read the court order; he expected the feds would take the case. "We plan to charge Mr. Riati with the murder of the John Doe, killed in the explosion off Staten Island."

"We are claiming jurisdiction for that murder inasmuch as it occurred in navigable waters of the United States."

Two U.S. Marshalls cuffed Freddy Riati and marched him out of the police station and into a waiting Chevy Suburban.

At the arraignment in U.S. District Court, Freddy pleaded not guilty on all charges. Jody Frank, Esq. asked for bail in the amount of $1,000,000. Bail was denied.

Jody Frank requested a meeting in chambers. The two attorneys met in Judge Wagoner's chambers.

"Well, councilor, why did you request this meeting." Judge Trent Wagoner was old, yet a long way from stepping down from the bench. He had worked his way up from public defender, to assistant district attorney, to a judge for the state of New Jersey, to judge for the U.S. District of New Jersey. He broached no nonsense in his courtroom, yet fairly applied the law and the rules. He had an encyclopedic memory on constitutional and procedural law.

Jody Frank, Esq. was undaunted. "Your honor the government has charged my client with the murder of the John Doe that was on his boat in 1990…"

"Yes?" Judge Wagoner was curious, waiting for Ms. Frank to get to the point.

"Well, your honor. The defense will take the position that the John Doe was already dead when the boat exploded and that my client is in no way responsible for his death."

"How do you know this, Miss Frank?"

"My client disclosed this to me, your honor. He found the body of a homeless man under an overpass in Trenton."

"Your honor, you can't allow this." Blake Jacoby had risen from his chair and was angry.

"Sit down. You will restrain yourself in my chambers and in my courtroom. There will be decorum maintained here.

"Yes, your honor. I'm sorry, sir. If I may."

"Calmly." The judge maintained his composure with no signs of agitation at this outburst in his chambers.

"Your honor, councilor is making an *ipse dixit* assertion. It's the word of a man who defrauded millions from his clients and faked his own death. I hope that you will quash this line of defense.

The judge turned his gaze from Blake Jacoby to Jody Frank. "Ms. Frank, I will allow you to make the claim to the jury, however, you will have to present evidence to back up your client's claim. Since it is your client who is the source for this, how will you submit proof unless you put your client on the stand? I grant this, not because I believe it is credible, but because I will not subject the decisions of this court to reversible error no matter how unlikely."

"Mr. Jacoby, you will have your opportunity to refute this claim. As you pointed out, the defendant's credibility is tenuous at best. That is all." With that Judge Wagoner arose. The chambers were emptied.

At trial, defense council argued in opening remarks that the body that was destroyed in the explosion was already dead.

The forensics expert at trial explained that the femur was consistent with Freddy Riati's height.

"Can you say with certainty that the body was alive before the explosion?" Jody Frank was not giving up on her claim and, short of putting Freddy on the stand, this was the only avenue left for her to cast doubt in the jury's mind.

"There was not enough tissue to perform any test to be certain the body was alive. Because there was no tissue it can't be known when the body had died.

"So the John Doe may have been dead when the boat exploded. Is that correct?"

"There was tissue attached to the femur that was found at the scene. That tissue had cells attached that were recently living cells. This evidence suggests the body was alive at the time of the explosion."

"Suggests. But doesn't prove."

"It's pretty clear the body was alive just before the explosion."

"Nothing further. Your honor, defense requests a recess."

"Court is adjourned until one o'clock." Judge Wagoner gaveled the proceedings to a close.

Turning to Blake Jacoby, she announces, "Can we meet?"

"Let's adjourn to a conference room."

"Give me a couple of minutes with my client."

Once the room is cleared, Jody Frank turns to Freddy. "This is not going well for you. The jury will convict you unless we can make a deal."

"What kind of deal?"

"Anything you have to give the prosecutor. Anything."

Freddy thinks for a minute.

"I'm not sure…"

"If a guilty verdict is returned you may spend the next 20 years in prison. And that's only if the sentences for the fraud and murder are served concurrently. If the sentences are consecutive you may spend the rest of your life behind bars."

"There were some who received some of the monies I took."

"Names. You will have to give them names or there will be no deal."

"Well, there's Carlos…"

"Your brother?"

"That's how he kept his business going. He almost went under in '89."

"How much?"

"Carlos?"

"Yeah, Carlos." She was impatient now.

"Over all…about a million."

Freddy Riati gave up his brother and three other prominent investment bankers in New Jersey. The prosecutor reduced the murder charge to desecration of a human corpse to be served concurrently with the fraud charge.

Freddy was given fifteen years in prison; Carlos was given ten years; and the two others were given ten years.

The parrot: he got the death sentence.

The P.I. Whose Name Was Charlie

Charlie Clark was a private investigator in
Hollywood. He'd done a lot and seen a lot. This day
in 1959, an unusual client walks into his office and
hires him to tail his wife. He takes the job, gets
roughed up along the way and solves two mysteries.

I arrived at my office at nine o'clock and had been at my desk for twenty, thirty minutes. With my feet on the desk, leaning back in my chair I was contemplating the rubber band that was wound around my left hand, the rubber band being the lotus transforming me to forgetfulness.

The elevator having been broken for I-don't-know-how-long, I had walked the forty-one steps to the second floor. The iron banister painted a gory-hued brown with worn spots of green peeking through, poorly complimented the gray walls, a testament to the faded glory of its heydays in 1920's Hollywood. The narrow hallway to my office with its rut filled wooden floor failed to add dignity to my surroundings. Perhaps this ambience was why I struggled to garner clients; this was within my budget and this was my digs.

It had been the middle of last week that I finished my last case – a "domestic" case. Husband suspected the little woman of an affair; turned out it was the guy's business partner. The client lost all the way around; the business was ruined and the marriage was on the rocks. I had the retainer in my pocket and though I felt bad for the guy and all he lost, I'd have felt worse if everything went bad for the guy *and* he owed me for my troubles to boot. I had a rent payment due that I wasn't sure I could make. The landlord let me delay some payments in the past, but they had become too frequent for his liking. Last month I had to let my secretary go – Doris. She was good and smart, typed a hundred-something words a minute and able to elicit information through a phone call – a swell asset that I miss greatly, as if I'd lost an appendage. A tall slender woman with fire-red hair. Now I was scraping by and I needed a client – bad.

Charlie Clark was a gumshoe. A private dick. A P.I. He was competent if not wholly on the straight and narrow. He was pertinacious in pursuit of his client's interests, though. His cases were mostly domestic: wife cheating on the husband; husband cheating on the wife, that sort of thing. Occasionally some retailer would have him sniffing around to find who was lifting cash or merchandise from the store owner. Charlie wasn't a snappy dresser; his suits hung limp on his lean, tall frame and his shoes rarely had a shine. What he lacked in appearance he made up for in determination.

Charlie's office is on the second floor of a four story commercial brick building on Fairfax Avenue, not far from Canter's deli. His was a place you had to look for to find. He had enough business to pay the bills and eat; not enough to get rich. Charlie had a dislike for the Hollywood types, especially the studio brass. Some of the movie people were ok – down to earth, alot of 'em, but he had a disdain for the casting-couch antics of some in the business.

He had his share of run-ins with the local police and spent a few nights in the crowbar hotel. The worst tangle he ever found himself in was the wife of a car dealer was found murdered. Charlie was hired by the owner to tail his wife, whom the owner suspected of having an affair. Boy did the hubby have that one figured. When she ended up with a fatal dent in her skull, the owner – husband – was the prime suspect. It was soon found that the suspect pool had expanded when it was learned the lady had been affectionately generous with several – and I mean *several* - gents around Hollywood. Turned out the culprit was a mechanic at the dealership; the guy was upset the lady closed the candy store on him. The cops wanted to know Charlie's involvement and the name of his client. Nothin' doin'. Charlie played his cards close to the vest and played along to get whatever information he could from the detectives. A grease stain on the lady's silk stockings sent Charlie to the dealership; time cards of the help found the mechanic with no alibi. Charlie "persuaded" the guy to come clean. His effort, however, was not met with the gratitude of the cops. Lead detective had his mug in the morning papers, telling how his smart work cracked the case.

Anyway.

I had been at my desk a while and was about to go out for coffee when a shadow appears at the door – one of those wood framed doors with a glass insert and my name on it: "Charlie Clark, P.I."

My hope had always been that a Jane Mansfield knock off would come through my door, a knock-out gorgeous brunette that turns every man's head. As I get up from my chair, the door opened and a rugged looking man entered; he couldn't have been five feet short. He wore a three piece suit and a slender, white necktie. The tie was held in place by a stick pin with a diamond that looked to be a full karat. The shoes were patent leather. The gent even had a cane – a short cane to be sure.

As I look down at him he says, "Four-Five."

Puzzled, I ask, "What?"

"I'm four foot, five inches tall," he replies. The voice was high pitched but projected with confidence.

I extend my hand. "I'm Charlie Clark. Please have a seat."

The fellow climbs into the chair on the other side of my desk and introduces himself.

"I'm Philip Darneaus. D-a-r-n-e-a-u-s, pronounced 'Dar No.' I want to hire you to tail my wife. I think she's seeing someone."

"I can help with that. Do you have a picture of your wife, Mr. Darneaus?"

Mr. D reaches in his suit jacket and pulls out a three by five photograph and hands it across the desk. "Her name is Phillis; a towering beauty."

The picture is of an attractive, well-built woman – if you get my meaning. Towering she's not. "How tall is she, Mr. Darneaus?"

"Four-eight!" he says with great excitement.

Phillis was posed with one hand on her hair, a model's or an actress's pose. She wore a white dress with puffy sleeves and a low cut neck, the kind that portrayed her rather immense virtues. She was a doll alright.

"How long have you suspected her of seeing someone?" I ask.

"She's been acting strangely for four, maybe five weeks. She doesn't come home right away every so often, about an hour late. She won't tell me where she's been," Mr. D declares.

"What does she say when you ask?" I ask.

"I don't ask," he says. "We've been married nearly twenty years and there's a trust between us. I'm just not sure, though."

"My fee is two hundred and fifty per day, plus expenses. I'll need a retainer of four days before I'll take the case."

The client jumps off the chair, reaches for his wallet and lays ten one hundred dollar bills on my desk and walks toward the door.

"One second," I interject. "Where can I find Miss Phillis?"

"At the studio. Where else?" he retorts.

"That narrows it, but only a little. Which studio?" I ask.

"M-G-M. It's been almost twenty years since 'Oz' and they still hire us," he says.

With that he's out the door.

Five minutes later I'm on the street and in my DeSoto. It's pretty, this car. Two-tone gray over gray; 1955. Rides like a dream.

I drive south on Fairfax to Beverly Boulevard, turn east toward Culver City; at Laurel Canyon Road I turn south and end up outside the M-G-M studio. I park and walk to the guard building. Eddy is on duty; I have spent time greasing palms with the various studio guards over the years and am on good terms with them.

"Eddy! Busy day?"

Eddy stands up straight, exits the guard building and shakes my hand.

"Charlie, it's been a while. Yeah, busy. They're working on some movie from back in Jesus' day. Chariots and horses; a big deal. That's about all I can say – that's about all I know. Heston's the big cheese in it. Blockbuster, they claim. We'll see. What brings you around?"

"Eddy, what can you tell me about Philip and Phillis Darneaus?"

"That couple is straight as they come! They've been here a long time. Nice as can be. Why? Any trouble there?"

"No, not really. Any problems with 'em?"

"Like I say, 'straight as they come.'"

"Are they on the lot?"

"Charlie, you're askin' a lot of questions. What gives?"

"Just looking into a domestic issue. Anything you can tell me? Do they come together to the studio? Leave together?"

"No," Eddy says, then pauses. "He has a chauffeur and she drives her own car, a specially rigged Caddy, you know, cuz she's so short. Pink with a lot of fluff in the interior. He leaves early afternoon and she leaves promptly at five. They both head north, up Laurel Canyon, got a place up there somewhere."

"Funny thing though," Eddy continued. "I've seen her take out of here and go east. Don't know why though, been doing that occasionally for about a month – maybe a little longer."

I continued with small talk, then got back in my car and sat. I didn't bother asking about the limo service, but might check into that angle later; if she was straying there could be a reason. It was just after noon and Phillis, the towering beauty, wouldn't be leaving for some time. East of the studio was an awful lot of playground: downtown LA, Lafayette Park, Southern Cal University. If one went east, then north there were hotels, clubs, and restaurants. I hoped to find out in which sandbox she played.

I returned to my office to contemplate the rubber band. There wasn't much to do until Phillis left the studio.

I drove back to the studio and parked just before five. In little less than five minute I spot Phillis and her Caddy exit the lot heading east. The caddy was a Coupe, white over pink with white side-walled tires and lots of chrome. I followed at a nice distance as she drove east on Pico then north on Vermont. She turned west on Wilshire and pulled into the Ambassador Hotel parking lot. The valet took her car. I began taking pictures of Phillis as a man greeted her at the door. The image in the view finder suddenly went black.

"Huh?" I uttered.

At that moment the camera was snatched from my hand and a very large fist reached in the driver's side window and took me by the collar of my coat; I was bodily removed from my car through the window and deposited on the pavement. I looked up to see a large man – a body-builder type – staring down at me.

"What's your business following Miss Darneaus, bub?" the guy asks.

Standing Homo-erectus and smoothing my jacket – as best as could be done – I looked up at the man.

"I'm a detective," I said.

"Yeah? Let's see your shield," he replied.

I produced my license and showed it to him.

"You ain't a detective, you're a P.I.," he spat.

"I've been hired to tail her," I explained.

"By who?" he asked.

"Whom."

"What?" he asked looking puzzled.

"It's 'By whom,'" I stated.

"You bein' cute, bub?" He grabbed me by my throat.

"I can't talk," I gasped. He released his grip.

"I can't tell you my client's name; it's protected by law"

"Yeah?"

"Yeah," I replied. "Who are you and what's your stake in this?"

"I'm a studio cop. It's my job to watch out for the studio people. Every once in a while some fan waits across the street from the studio, then follows one of the stars; it's become a big problem. My job is to step in and protect the studio people."

"I'm not out to harm Mrs. Darneaus. I'm just watching. She lives up in the canyon, right?

"Hey, what are you trying to pull here? I ain't telling you that. I hear any harm comes to the lady, I'll be lookin' for you. Ya hear me?"

"I hear you. I'm not here to hurt the lady, see?" I reach in my jacket pocket and pull out one of my cards and hand it to him.

He inspected the card, put it in the chest pocket of his shirt and left. I walked across the street and into the Ambassador.

This was only the second time I'd been here and was equally impressed this time with the magnificent entrance, the fireplace and chandeliers, the place reeking of money and power, a playpen for the glamorous. The denizen of the Ambassador were the well-heeled, the influential, the moguls, the movers and shakers of the film and entertainment industry.

No sooner had I crossed the entryway than my path was blocked by a tall, muscular man wearing a ruffled shirt and a vest.

"Where you goin', bub?"

Is everyone 'bub'? Sizing him up, I hesitated, then gave him my most disarming smile.

"I'm going in to have some coffee."

"No you ain't, not dressed like that," sayeth the gorilla.

I looked myself over and straightened my tie.

"What's wrong with how I'm dressed?"

"You look like you slept in that suit, bub. Maybe you should go across the street to The Derby; they'll serve you over there."

Just then I see the lady approaching; she'd been there fifteen minutes, tops. I plan my exit.

"Eh, yeah. You're right. Sorry for the trouble."

I turned around just after Phillis passes me and watch as her car was brought up. I scramble to my car and follow her out Wilshire Boulevard to Laurel Canyon Road. At this point I figure she's headed for home, so I break off my tail and go home.

I contemplate the case over a bologna sandwich and a beer, a few beers.

Phillis wasn't in the Ambassador long enough to have an affair, but there was a reason for her to go out of her way. I just didn't know the reason – yet.

The next morning I had breakfast at a diner and headed to my office. I prepared to type my notes on the previous day's events, having inserted the paper, placed the cursor and about to type. I see a miniature shadow at the door and a visibly angry Philip Darneaus enters.

"What am I paying you for? You're hired to protect my wife and she gets cut off on Laurel Canyon Road!" Mr. D screams.

I try my best to calm him and ask him to sit; he's having none of it. Philip is beyond being calmed.

"Philip," I said in my calmest voice, an effort to relax him. "I want you to remember that I wasn't hired to protect Phillis; I was hired to find out if she was seeing someone. I don't know what happened, so why don't you tell me. What happened on Laurel?"

Mr. D calmed a little and, looked around found a chair and climbed into it.

"She was on her way home last night – about 5:15 or 5:30 – and she's hit by another vehicle and driven off the road."

"Is Phillis hurt?" I asked.

"No, except for a few bruises."

"Was her car damaged?"

"Left front fender. It's in the shop.

"Did she see the other vehicle?" I asked.

"Yeah. She says it was an old pickup. Blue-green and white. Ford." Philip says.

"Did she see the driver?"

"No, but he stopped after the crash; he was wearing a black cowboy hat. She said she didn't see the driver's face."

"Do you know exactly where it happened?"

Philip hesitated, then rubbed his chin. "I think so."

Philip and I climbed into my car and we headed over to Laurel Canyon Road. We find pieces of Phillis' car and pull off the road. I pulled a tape measure from the glove box and walked to the start of the skid marks.

"Philip, hold this end of the tape measure. Here, at the skid marks."

I walked off the marks. Exactly eighty feet. I write it in my note pad. We walk past where Phillis' car stopped and see a second set of marks and we repeat the procedure. Two hundred eighty feet.

I noticed a broken headlight that didn't look like it was from a caddy; likely from the pickup.

We return to my car and I make some calculations.

"The car that struck Phillis' was doing seventy-five; she was doing forty. I don't know if that tells us much, but the driver stopped for a reason; maybe he was looking to see if Phillis was ok. This could have been a target or it could have been a drunk driver. The time fits for a drunk driver, an afternoon cocktail – or a few – and a drive home.

We returned to my office. I assured Philip I would look into this along with the matter of whether Phillis was seeing someone. Philip left, calmer than when he arrived.

I drove over to the studio to talk with Eddy.

"Charlie, I didn't expect to see you so soon. What's up?" Eddy asks.

"Eddy, can you get me some biographical information on the Darneaus couple?" I ask.

Without a word, Eddy picks up the phone and dials.

"Hey, I got a fellow wants a bio sheet on Philip and Phillis Darneaus. Can you send someone over to the guard shack with it? Yeah. Thanks."

"They'll pull it out of the files and bring it," Eddy says.

"There was a crash on Laurel Canyon last night. Phillis Darneaus was banged up. Did she arrive today?" I asked.

"Yeah. She was bruised all right. Studio sent some make up people over to fix her up; she has a shoot today. Why you askin'? What happened?"

I responded to his questions, "I guess she was run off the road up on Laurel Canyon. Someone in an older Ford pickup driving at a pretty good clip, too.

We continued with some small talk.

In what seemed to be half an hour a lady walks to the guard building with the information. She hands it to Eddy; Eddy hands it to me. I left for my office to look over the information.

Back at my office, I'm digesting the information. Much of it highlights from the movies in which they've appeared, plus birth dates, Zodiac signs, the date they were married, newspaper clippings. No children. Blah, blah, blah.

I put the papers on my desk and return to my rubber band.

I decided to drive over to the body shop and have a look at the car.

As I walked in I was greeted by a short Hispanic man.

"What can I do for you, senor?" He asks as he ponders my car.

"I'm an insurance investigator," I said. "I'm here to examine the pink caddy belonging to Mrs. Darneaus."

"Eets parked in the lot, senor," he says and leads me around the building to the car.

I examined the front driver's side fender and note the turquoise paint left by the pickup. The marks were thirty-four inches off the pavement.

"I'm looking for a turquoise and white Ford pickup with damage to the front fender, passenger's side. If you see it, give me a call," I said as I hand him my card.

"Si, senor."

It was still early afternoon so I drove over to the Ambassador. I drove around to the back in time to see some trucks lined up. One was from a company that manages stage and sound productions. Seeing one man with a clip board in one hand and a pen in the other, I approached him with my business card in my left hand and my open right hand extended to greet him. He shakes my hand then examines the card.

"Good afternoon," I began as I looked around in my most officious manner. "I'm Charlie Clark, security. Is everything ok?"

The man looked at me with a puzzled countenance.

"I'm Jimmy Getz. Yes, everything is fine. Say, this must be a big deal if security is looking over the delivery of the sound and stage equipment. It's going swell," he said. "Rumor has it Cugat's band is playing in the Grove for some shindig Saturday night. Guy inside says the place will be packed – and it's a closed party; somebody bought the whole place for the night!"

"That's why I'm here, to make sure there's no foul-up," I said. "Make sure everything is first rate here, ok?"

"Yes sir," Jimmy said.

Not sure what I just learned or what it has to do with the Darneaus couple. I left and checked out a few body shops for damaged Ford pickups. Nothing. Late afternoon, I head for home to a hot meal: peanut butter toast. And beer.

In the morning, I went to the office and reexamined the biographical information on the Darneaus couple. After a brief glance, I tossed in on the desk; the papers scattered, one falling to the floor. Frustrated, I lumbered around the desk to retrieve the paper. It was a news clipping on the wedding. May 9, 1941 was the date line. The marriage of Philip Darneaus and Phillis Rafertty in Burbank, California. The luminaries were many, mostly cast members from Oz.

The couple met during the filming and became an item; they were inseparable. That was eighteen years ago – this Saturday.

On a hunch, I opened the Yellow Pages to 'florists' and started dialing.

"Hello, I'm calling to check on the order for the Darneaus Wedding Anniversary. Can you tell me if the order will be filled on time? The party is Saturday at the Ambassador. No? I'm so sorry."

Many more calls netted the same result. Finally I hit pay dirt.

"Yes? The flowers will be delivered Saturday by noon? Please confirm the spelling. Yes, D-a-r-n-e-a-u-s. Thank you so much."

I slumped in my chair and let all the air out of my lungs in one burst.

I drove to the studio and handed Eddy a note for Phillip. It being Friday, I could give him the information and put one part of my case behind me; I would still pursue the hit and run.

Back at my office, I began typing my final report of Phillis Darneaus. At three-fifteen, the door opens and in walks Philip.

"Please have a seat," I asked.

Philip climbs into a chair and looks at me with trepidation.

"Philip," I began, "rest easy. Phillis is not seeing anyone. Her activities over the past four, five weeks will become evident soon – and to your great pleasure. I won't have the final report ready until Monday afternoon, but know that she has not been seeing anyone."

"But those times she would come home late…"

I cut him off.

"You will know the answer to that soon. For now, go home and enjoy your weekend."

"She's wanting us to go to the Coconut Grove tomorrow night. It's our anniversary. I'll take your advice and try to forget my fears and doubts. She's been a wonderful partner for, what, eighteen years. If you're sure."

"I'm sure – certain. I will find out about the crash, if you want."

He became animated.

"Yes, I want you to find out who hurt my Phillis! I want that person to go to jail!"

It took some time to calm him and assure him that I would continue to pursue the crash. He left my office in better spirits than when he arrived.

I arose from my chair and walked across the room to the window facing the street. Phillip exited the building as his driver opened the rear door of the limousine. The car drove off.

I began to close the curtain when I saw an older Ford pickup, turquoise and white, parked on Oakwood at Fairfax in the next block. How many could there be?

I locked my office door and exited the building. As I turned to where the truck was parked, it pulled away, driving past me; damaged right front fender. I jumped in the DeSoto and followed the truck as it turned east on Rosewood, then south on Highland before turning east on Beverly Boulevard, turned into the parking lot of a cocktail lounge. I parked in the adjacent spot.

"Man, that's a great looking truck. What year is it?" I asked.

"'53," he said.

"Looks good," I said. "What happened to the front fender?"

"I hit a tree," he said. Laughing, "Damn thing jumped in front of me! Ha ha!"

He held the door for me and we sat next to one another at the bar.

"What'll you have," the barkeep asks me.

"A short beer," I said.

"The usual?" he asked 'crash.'

"Yeah."

"I'm Charlie," I said. "Charlie Clark," as I extended my hand.

"I'm Joey Short," the driver of the pickup said. Joey had a smooth complexion with black hair and long sideburns. He was no taller or shorted that Charlie – five-ten. He wore a black western hat, a white t-shirt with a pack of cigarettes rolled up in one sleeve, denim jeans with the pant legs turned up and western boots. He spoke with a west Texas drawl, whether real or put-on.

The bartender brought me my beer and places two shot glasses and a tall beer in front of Joey.

"Here's to ya," he said, looking at me. He emptied the first of the shot glasses followed by most of the beer. "Ahhh!" He downed the second shot glass and the last of the beer. "One more, Mike," he said.

Mike, the barkeep brought him another set of drinks.

"You're mighty thirsty," I said.

"He does this every day," Mike offered. "Comes in about 3:30-4:00 and has six or eight drinks then he's gone."

Joey drank two more rounds then heads to the restroom.

"That's a great looking truck he's got," I commented.

Mike's brow furrowed, "He was sure sore last night when he came in. Said he hit a tree after he left here the night before. I guess I'm not surprised as much as he drinks."

I thanked him for the beer, bade my goodbyes and left.

Well, Charlie filled out his report on Monday and presented it to Phillip. Charlie called the detective working the case on the hit and run, giving the police Joey's name and the license plate number of the Ford F100 pickup.

That Saturday night, May 9, 1959, Hollywood saw one of the biggest soirees ever. Every A-lister in the business was at the Coconut Grove, as was studio brass, producers and directors. The music business was there too: Frank, Dean, Sammy, Miss Day, and Miss Page. Xavier Cugat – and Charo – performed. It was a gala to rival Oscars night.

As if it were scripted, one more person was in attendance: M-G-M stunt man, Joey Short. Joey was drunk.

The 1920's In a Blur

He was a man living in times both exciting and evil, a man caught up in the spirit of his age. He drank to excess and the only lover he knew suddenly was gone. This man, timid in so many ways, became energized when he was with Angie and was made more alive in her presence.

We – some, not all – had survived influenza of 1918-1919 and there was a new expectation. After seeing so many around us die, we thirsted for signs that we were alive, something exhilarating. And what did we do? We passed the Volstead Act which began prohibition. Perhaps the only ones who truly favored this were the gangsters and mobsters; they cleaned up plenty. The speakeasies opened; the illegal breweries opened; and booze was brought down from Canada or from the Caribbean through the Great Lakes. The G-men tried their best to do their jobs and one wonders how many of them thought it a doleful task. They did it well, however, dumping hundreds, maybe thousands of gallons of alcohol into the sewers.

In spite of prohibition it was a time of great jazz music and gaiety. Around the University of Chicago campus, young men, students tall and refined dressed in expensive suits and wore spats with homburg or panama hats; the ladies, slender and beautiful wore beaded evening dresses or drop-waist dresses, hung straight on their bodies. The skirts were short and the shoes were strap heeled shoes matching the color of their dresses. For overcoats the women wore full length fur collared wrap coats or full length fur coats; the men also wore long fur-collared coats. Summer ware was lighter, both in weight and in color – most especially in springtime.

I grew up in the Hyde Park area, a tony section on Chicago's south side. One didn't root for the Cubs if you lived south of Madison Street or the White Sox if you lived north. It was only a short while since The Scandal of the 1919 World Series but we were still Sox fans. Joe Jackson was gone the following year and the White Sox struggled.

Shea Donally was my best friend; we went to school together until we turned fourteen. When he was fourteen he took a job running errands for Patrick Reilly. Mr. Reilly was known throughout the neighborhood as a mob guy – THE mob guy. Shea started out running errands, then collected money for Mr. Reilly. By the time he was twenty, Shea was wearing nice suits and had lots of money. When prohibition came, he was running one of the speakeasies. He had become a hard character, Shea. It was reported that one customer at his club got drunk and became too handsy with one of the ladies. Shea kicked the side of the gent's knee and the guy crumpled to the floor. Shea grabbed the guy by the back of his jacket and dragged him into the alley, then worked him over. The drunk fellow never came back I was told. Mostly Shea's joint was well mannered with a wealthy clientele.

So, one afternoon, I walked into the place. The music, the smoke and the smells were electrifying. The band was playing *Ain't We Got Fun* followed by Jolson's *O-H-I-O* and the dance floor was packed. Every song they played was a current hit; they were great! Standing at the bar I ordered a Rob Roy and who was it that embraced me but Shea? We gave each other a bear hug that seemed to last a long time. Taking a step back, Shea's grin was longer than the Magnificent Mile. "I haven't seen you in, I don't remember when. What are you doing these days?"

"You look like a million bucks, Shea. Wow! It has been a long time. I'm finishing my studies at the University of Chicago. I'm studying accounting and soon will have my CPA license."

"I knew you were destined for big things. Say, when you graduate and get that license, come back here for a celebration. I can find a place for you in the organization. I guarantee you'll make a bunch of money."

Shea looked around the room and, noticing a tall girl with a draping body-fit dress and ear rings dangling from tiny ears. He beckoned.

"Beatrice! Over here."

She strode across the floor smooth as a dancer.

"Yes Mr. Donally?"

"Beatrice, this is my friend. I want you to give him whatever he wants. On me."

"Sure thing, Mr. Donally," she said.

Turning to me she asked, "What would you like, sugar?"

"Well, I still have some of my Rob Roy. A refill would be nice," I said as I downed the rest of my drink and handed her my glass.

And so it went. After a few drinks I left – a little light headed but not out of control. It was a long time after that day until I saw Shea again

I got my ticket to practice accounting and did all right – not great but all right. I took a job at Calumet National in '21. The bank was busy. Folks had come home from the war and were buying up houses and cars. Nobody seemed to care how much the house cost, they just got bought up. It wasn't unusual for a recently returning veteran to borrow two grand or more to buy a house.

In the summer of '23 I dropped by Shea's place again. This time, I took the job and, boy was I busy. I don't know where the money came from but there was a lot of it. Well, yes I do know the source of the money. The money was washed through various legitimate businesses owned by Patrick Reilly. I knew about it, yet I didn't know – if you know what I mean. I was just an employee. As long as the money could be accounted for legitimately, I didn't care. Oh, and it was a not-so-quiet rumor that Shea had become a button man as well as the guy running the club. I didn't care to hear the details. I didn't mind doing what I was doing but I didn't want anything to do with any killings. Shea was my friend, but when it comes to killing the friendship is pretty thin.

And they kept me in free drinks. That was a constant. I hung out at the club and was given free drinks, then in the morning when the place closed I took care of the books. I was included in Shea's private parties too.

"C'mon, have yourself one of these dames."

"Ah, Shea, I'm fine with sitting and drinking my gin."

"Bobbie is a doll and she's ready to party. Have a go with her."

I poured some more gin, shook my head and raised my glass. Oh, and Bobby, she was a doll alright, but I knew that eventually this – with the women – could get men into fights and arguments or worse. I stayed away from it and lived to not regret it.

Then in '24 young Bobby Franks was murdered. He was just a kid, fourteen they reported. It was told that two fellows from the neighborhood had killed Bobby. Shea and I both knew the families. The families were well off, and I mean *well* off. The guys from the neighborhood, Nathan Leopold and Richard Loeb, lured Bobby into their car then killed him. They drove into Indiana with the kid on the floor of the back seat and ate a hot dog while they waited for the sun to go down. They hid Bobby's body in a culvert and, in the process, Nathan lost a pair of glasses – the kind that was expensive and that only a few had been made. Oh, and these geniuses couldn't hide the body for longer than a few hours.

Some guy saw Bobby's legs sticking out of the culvert the next morning. When they found the glasses at the scene, the cops checked out the ophthalmologists that sold them and got a list of buyers. Everyone could account for their glasses except Leopold. Nathan was taken in for questioning and, when he said he was with Richard, both were questioned. They claimed they were in Nathan's car in a park trying to pick up a couple of girls. Their alibi broke down quickly because the car they claimed they were driving that afternoon was being repaired by the Leopold family chauffer.

They confessed. The prosecutor was pleased that he had a sure death sentence case, at least until the opening of the trial when Judge Caverly allowed any motions to be presented by either the prosecution or the defense. Well, Darrow stood up and announced that the defendants wished to change their plea to 'guilty.' The prosecution was stunned, realizing that without the jury to render a verdict and a recommendation for sentencing, these men would not receive the punishment that most folks in Chicago thought they deserved.

Nathan Leopold and Richard Loeb were sent to prison, each for life plus ninety-nine years. The Daily News covered the story from the time the ransom was demanded until the trial. And boy did they want blood. It seemed like everyone wanted these two to hang. Folks were sure sore when the judge let 'em off easy.

And the band played on. The music was magic and the bands were spectacular. Ma Rainey came to town with Louis Armstrong, riding a string of hits. And the liquor flowed. Shea sprung for a Ford Model "A" convertible cabriolet and took me for a ride. Every head turned to see his very long automobile with the top down and going faster than anything on the road. Gone were the days when a Ford came in only black, this one was red – and boy did it look good. When he stepped on the accelerator it got up to sixty miles an hour!

I was making six figures then and wearing nice clothes. I moved out of my folks' house and bought my own. The house was a small two bedroom house; it wasn't much, but it was mine.

That was the year I met Angie. Angie was stunningly beautiful with a wonderfully, gay smile. She was the archetype of the 20's, alive in every way. When she tilted her head back and laughed, it was captivating. Everyone loved Angie and I was her fella. She was the most beautiful girl ever and I was happy – happy like I'd never been.

That year Angie and I spent celebrating; we were alive and wanted the world to know it. We feasted on each other, and in every way. We went to the best clubs and restaurants in town. We enjoyed the lavish chop houses and the oyster bars located in the Loop. Henrici's on Randolph Street was our favorite; they had an international menu prepared by European chefs. We loved each other with gusto, whether we were out on the town or in our bed. We were the epitome of the Roaring 20's.

In '25 I found it difficult to keep up with Angie. She had a level of energy that was unattainable by my best efforts. When I wearied and had to sleep, she continued to hunger life without me. It was on one summer day that year that I first saw her using cocaine.

"What is that, Angie?"

"It's cocaine. Try some."

No! Don't do that. I don't like you to use that."

"Dearest, it makes me feel so alive. I can do anything. I'm ready to dance," she said as she twirled in place. "You have to get ready. It's almost six. I wanna dance."

"Ok. I'll get ready."

Quick as I could I got ready. It was half past six when we left her place and drove to Sean's. We were there an hour when a bell sounded.

"What's that?" I was frantic not knowing what was happening.

"It's the alarm. The feds are coming. Quick, behind the bar is a stairway to the cellar."

We ran around the bar and followed some of the help down to the cellar. From there we walked through a tunnel that came out in the basement of a bakery. We ascended the stairway into the bakery, then out the back door. Sean locked the door. He didn't seem upset by all this.

"They'll smash everything."

"Sean, you'll be ruined."

Sean and I were leaning against the alley wall of the bakery. He handed me a smoke and then broke into laughter.

"How can you laugh?"

Angie joined in the laughter.

"The feds'll bust up the place all right. In a couple of days it'll be open again."

"What?" I stammered.

"She's right. I make enough on this operation that this is only a mild setback. In three days I'll be open again. Let's go find a drink."

We walked the twelve blocks to another of Patrick Reilly's clubs. Mr. Reilly was there that night and Sean explained what had happened. All was good, Mr. Reilly said. Just a cost of doing business.

Being this was Mr. Reilly's prime club the music was better and the band was bigger. Angie and I danced until the place shut down the next morning. Before we left she made a stop in the restroom. Tired when she went in, she was energetic when she came out.

The rest of the year she continued in her life's celebration, except the lack of sleep began to take a toll on her looks. Two days before Christmas 1925 Angie, exhausted and drunk, passed out on a Chicago street. She never awakened.

I mourned her death in the only way I knew: I drank myself into a stupor. For two days I didn't eat and barely slept; passed out is more like it. Then I would wake up and pour another drink. Shea pounded on my door one afternoon. I could barely make it to the door and when I opened it I slumped to the floor. He picked me up and slapped me. He slapped me around good until I could focus my eyes on him.

"You gonna kill yourself like this! You gotta stop. I need you to help me, to do some work for me. I can't run my operation without you."

"Uh, wait," was all I could say.

Shea slapped me once again. It stung, where he slapped me. I saw two of him and they never came into focus. His words were loud and hurt my ears.

"Ok. Ok. Don't hit me anymore. I lost my Angie," I sobbed as I raised my hands to cover my face.

He dragged me to the bathroom and ran hot water in the tub.

"Take yourself a bath, shave and put some clothes on," he ordered.

In half an hour I was looking mostly alive again and in his car. I slumped back in the seat as he drove. We drove to the club and he ordered me to account for the money for the last three days. I worked at it slowly, nodding off from time to time, but managed to record all the money by eight o'clock that night. Shea ordered me to go home, get some sleep and – most of all – to stay out of the bottle.

When I got home, I was too exhausted to have a drink or eat; I laid on the bed, in my street clothes, and went to sleep.

Next afternoon when I went to work the girls were really nice to me. Maybe they were the night before except I didn't notice. They all expressed sympathy for me as they knew that Angie and I had been an item. I put my head on one of the girls' shoulder and cried. This was the only time I cried over Angie. She didn't say a word, the girl, just stroked my back.

I stopped drinking that winter. It was different. I forgot what it was like not living in a fog. Except one night the club had a terrific haul. It was St. Patrick's Day, March 17, 1926. To be honest the celebration only began on the 17th; it ended the morning of the 18th. Shea put a grand in my pocket and a high ball in my hand. I didn't get home until after noon and I crashed. That started the roller coaster again. It wasn't the kind of drinking like when Angie died but it was several drinks a day. I ate at Berghoff's or Workingman's Exchange. I could get a beer and a sandwich for ten cents.

Melody, one of the girls at the club, took me to her place after we closed one morning. She told me I looked like I hadn't eaten in a while, which was true enough. She fixed some potatoes and sausage. I devoured the meal. She only offered me water to drink. She didn't drink she said and I could sense that she didn't want for me to drink either. Don't get me wrong. She had no problem with the people at the club drinking, it was concern for my health I think was the reason she wished me not to drink.

"That was good, Melody," I said as I wiped my mouth. "Where'd you learn to cook like this?"

"At home," she replied in brief.

"Where's home?"

"A farm just south of Vandalia, Illinois."

"What's that?"

"Vandalia. It was once the capital of Illinois. Lincoln served there and his desk is a big deal. You can still visit there and see the desk."

"Oh," I said, not sure what else to say.

"Mom has been to the old capital building lots of times. She loves Lincoln. Best president since Washington, she says."

"Sounds nice," was all I could think of to say.

I saw Melody on and off throughout 1926. Not every day, understand, once or twice a week she would invite me to her place or I would take her to a movie. She laughed when Buster Keaton played *The General* with his herky-jerky walk; and the glitz and glamor of *Gatsby* sent her over the top! It seemed like in some ways we were living the Gatsby story. In some ways it reminded me of the parties with Shea, his friends, and the women. Mostly it reminded me of Angie, especially Jay's love for Daisy.

Then the Italians moved into the south side. Shea took a bullet to the shoulder when the Italians tried to kill him. The micks killed the Italians and the Italians killed the micks. Several of Shea's employees got roughed up or killed. A car careening around a corner sent people diving for the pavement or behind the closest door or car. Bullets sprayed like water from a broken fire hydrant and nobody was safe; it didn't matter who you were or whose side you were on, when bullets fly everyone is a target.

It became all-out war and I told Melody to high tail it back to the farm. I couldn't stay in Chicago any longer. One couldn't live on six figures if one were dead.

Melody went back home and I headed west. Past Denver, all the way to Los Angeles.

Los Angeles had its own form of corruption, I learned. Most of the girls were prettier than the Midwestern variety but not as friendly. Sunshine makes for a less pasty complexion but perhaps it gives one an inflated sense of importance.

I took a job with MGM in the accounting department. I was a part of a crew that dealt with the logistics of off-the-lot productions. This took me to places both beautiful and barren. I saw the leading men and women up close. The behind-the-scenes activities were surprising. What the publicists and the production company portrays is not exactly what goes one, if you know what I mean. Some of these ladies were dolls even without the make-up. One of the leading men was the hardest to get along with I've ever met, and I mean with everyone, top to bottom. People gave him a wide berth when he walked by. In the speakeasy everyone worked for one purpose: to make a buck; in Hollywood there seemed to be too many egos. They worked at making their films all right, but a few of 'em thought they were so much more important than the rest.

The producers and directors were on a schedule but the rest of the crew were just as interested in the after-shoot parties. And boy, were there parties. It didn't matter where the shoot was, they flew in cases of booze. Champagne was a must, but everything was there for the asking. As the accountant, I can tell you the studio picked up the tab.

It was magic what was done in film. If a sandstorm was needed, they'd truck in as much sand as there is on the beach at Santa Monica; snow, well that wasn't as real as was the sand. It was all make believe, same as some of the people. MGM made more than 40 films in '26 and had contracts with Garbo, Lionel Barrymore, and Lillian Gish. Lil was a doll, quiet and unbecoming, from a hard background too I was told.

Jill was different though. Jill worked in costumes, a real seamstress and a swell person. We had a relationship that was more down to earth than I had with Angie. She was from up around Bakersfield. Her family were farmers in the San Joaquin Valley and she learned her craft from her mother; all the clothes her family wore were hand-made and she loved the clothes from the past, whatever era. She could fit someone like a king or a pauper. What I liked best was she was smart. I don't know where she learned what she knew, but she knew a lot about a lot. We would talk for hours. She didn't drink, but didn't mind that I did. She just let me be me. She could talk about anything it seemed. She was the one who filled me in on all the folks on set. She knew the backgrounds of the folks on both sides of the camera: actors, actresses, prop men, electricians, or carpenters; she knew 'em all.

Jimmy Cramer was an aspiring actor. I liked Jimmy because he was down to earth. He was humble, I guess because he wasn't a big-shot star, just a bit actor. We'd hang around together after a shoot and visit. He liked my stories about Chicago and all the parties. He told me he wished he had known Angie because she seemed so alive. The girls all liked Jimmy because he was a terrific looking guy. Jill thought he was a great guy but wasn't taken in by his charming good looks. It seems she liked her men a bit less dazzling, kinda like me, I suppose.

This was 1927, a year that ended when the Parker twins were kidnapped. Well only one of the twins, Marion, was taken; Marjorie, for some reason was not taken. William Hickman waltzed into her junior high school and told the administrator that her father, Perry, was injured and needed to see his daughter. Perry was a bank employee at Security-First National Bank in Los Angeles. The girl was taken from her school and a $1500 ransom was asked – in gold, mind you. After receiving the money Hickman returned the girl – in pieces. Hickman had disarticulated and disemboweled young Marion, which shocked all of LA. The city want blood, let me tell you. He was caught within a week hiding out in Oregon, returned to Los Angeles, tried and convicted. Hickman's comment after the trial was that the state had won – by a neck. And it had, as William Hickman was hanged in San Quentin the following October.

Throughout 1928 Jill and I grew closer. I had never thought of marrying, but I did that summer. I think it would have worked too. It's possible I was afraid it wouldn't work out because I walked out. Left Jill. Left Hollywood. Left California.

I'm in Tijuana now living on the little money I've saved. I'm able to afford food, a daily newspaper and tequila.

The '20's was a time of revelry, of wonderful music, of glitz and glamor; it was also a time of horror. The mob wars, the Bobby Franks, and the Marion Parkers. How many more were like that? It can't even be said that it was the best of times and the worst of times. The best was good, but not the best. Those years, at times, approached the worst, though.

Then in '29 it all came crashing down, as it had to. After the flash, comes the dark. The flash was brilliant just as the dark was like an abyss.

I've spent most of my adult life in a daze. I don't say this out of regret because it's a comforting way to tread through life. Nothing much bothers me and nothing much matters.

I've contented myself with this dullness. It's easy.

The Institute

The Institute houses those people who refuse to assimilate into proper society. Two men, "clients" of The Institute, pledge to bring down the facility. This chronicles their efforts and explains their ethos.

I

The moment I met Timmy I knew he was smart. Not just intelligent, but wily – that kind of smart. We met in The Institution of Behavioral Conformity for the crime of insult, each having challenged authority and been adjudicated as requiring 'modification.'

Timmy had informed a teacher at the Mathematical Academy that a solution to a Cartesian graph was in error and, when she failed to see her error, he persisted. I only vaguely understood it when he told me; it was the placement of the axis of symmetry in a quadratic equation. For his insult, he was confined – indefinitely, mind you – to The Institute.

I have always been forceful; I argue for the sake of arguing and I was told – ordered – by a government clerk that I had to return with my business application the following day.

"But you're here now!" I replied. "I'm here now! All that's required is for you to take my application and hand it off to the proper person!"

Somewhere at her desk, she pressed a button and some burly men in uniform took me to a holding cell and, after a brief hearing, I was locked up.

At The Institute we shared a room that was nicely furnished with two beds, a desk and a shared closet. The walls were festooned with slogans, you know motivational crap! We could leave our room during the day and go to the common room which was decorated with more slogans, the kind whose purpose was to inform you of acceptable behavior. I knew all I needed about 'harmony' and 'cooperation' and the like. My point of contention was being confined for disagreement. We could not leave the building and we met daily with an 'arbitrator' whose duty was to assess our suitability to reenter society.

So Timmy, as I said, was smart. He was the sort who could assess a situation and adapt to it. He would do it and you would believe him. I don't say this lightly because he was a born actor and could convince you that, at twenty-four, he was an astrophysicist of some renown – or a priest, if there were such people anymore.

So we're meeting one afternoon with the 'arbitrator' and had this back and forth discussion – mostly forth. It would be unwise to disagree with the 'arbitrator' as she was in control of your fate. Anyway, about ten minutes before we were finished, Timmy shuffles a bit in his seat, lowers his head in a contrite manner and begins organizing the books in front of him, you know, he's stacking the four books he has been given on normative behavior.

"My father," he began, with a most dour countenance, "had always said I should be responsible, that duty was important. I have tried my best all my life to do that, be responsible. My mother taught me to be kind and respectful of everyone."

Timmy even had a tear or two in his eyes that he wiped with the back of his hand periodically.

"I know I have failed them and that I should honor those who have been given authority. I'm sorry," he said.

The 'arbitrator' positively beamed at him. I almost gagged because I knew it was garbage! It was obvious that it was working, though, and I didn't want to spoil it for Timmy.

"I really believe you mean that, Timmy," said the 'arbitrator.' "I think you have taken to heart all we have instilled in you. You are contrite, aren't you?"

With chest heaving and a deep sigh he replied, "Oh, yes. I have failed my fellow citizens and am so very sorry."

I had to suppress vomiting!

"I think you are ready to reenter society, Timmy," she said. "You will be released immediately."

With a stern look in my directions she berated me, "I only wish you had the smallest part of Timmy's remorse, Martin."

"I will be pleased to go with him, to see to it that he doesn't wander and fall into old habits," I replied.

"You may never be released."

"You may be right," I said. "I cannot understand how a society can indefinitely incarcerate someone for disagreeing with a public official. This is not new as infallibility of church officials was argued centuries ago. In some archives are twentieth century movies, one of which has an official – much like yourself – telling an inmate how the prison will help the inmate '…get his mind right.' Inasmuch as I refuse to yield to your efforts at my reeducation, I will never be released!"

II

We left the counselling session, along with the arbitrator. She stopped at her office to fetch the release papers for Timmy and signed them. We proceeded to our room where Timmy gathered his few belongings and he was escorted to the end of the hall. The guard at the exit door hardly looked up after noticing the arbitrator's white lab coat. Then, walking down the stairs and out the door, Timmy was gone.

My room seemed more barren than it had been before Timmy's departure. I pledged in that moment that I wasn't going to allow my solitude to shape me into conformity. I wasn't adept at theatrics in the way Timmy was and, so, I could not pull off his mode of exit.

Three days later, as I was laying across my bed, I heard a noise at the window. Looking toward the window I saw nothing and, so, I thought nothing of it. Then another sound. And another. I arose and looked out the window. Timmy was standing there waving both arms. Then, pointing at me, he made a jumping motion. He could see I was confused by what he was doing so he did it again. I mouthed the words, "Do you want me to jump?" He nodded his head up and down frantically. I examined the window casing but the window was imbedded in the concrete. The window would not permit me an exit. And then Timmy left.

For the next several days I thought about my escape. I felt that if I could conceive of a plan, I could be free of The Institute.

I remembered how it was that Timmy was let out. The facilitator – or rather the white lab coat of the facilitator – was all that was required to get past the guard.

During craft time, I hid a needle in my trousers along with a measure of white thread. Each day for the next two weeks I absconded with white thread. Each week I tore a length of my bedsheet so as to have white material with which to make my "lab coat." It wasn't elegant, the coat, but might pass the guard's scrutiny. I picked the lock on the supply room door and, once inside, I stole a clip board and some papers.

Donning my makeshift lab coat and with clipboard in hand I ambled to the exit. The guard hardly looked up from the paperback novel he was reading, nodded, and opened the exit door. I grunted as I passed through, walked down the one flight of stairs and was out the door.

I wandered through the area where I had seen Timmy but could not find him. I was ready to leave and go somewhere, anywhere, when I heard him.

"Psst! Martin! Over here."

"Where?" I asked looking around.

"Over here."

The sound's direction caused me to turn. Seeing Timmy was the happiest moment of my life. I couldn't believe that we were together – and away from The Institute.

"Come on," he said, "I've got a place not far from here."

He led me to a shack about a mile away. It was covered over with foliage such that one would never find it unless one was looking for it and knew where it was. There was a bog that nearly surrounded it making access difficult. We entered and sat. We just stared vacantly for a long time, until Timmy got up and put a pot of water on the little stove that was in the corner.

We said nothing while drinking tea. Then Timmy spoke.

"Martin," he said, looking more serious than I can ever remember. "Martin, what they did, what The Institute is, it's wrong. It should never exist and people like us should never face what we endured. Brainwashing is what it is. It's evil. We must stop it. We must end it. We must destroy it and bring it down."

"What are you talking about? 'Destroy it.' How? How can we do this?

"The first thing is, we have to get the others out. All of them. What 15-20 of 'em?

I was astounded. "Get them out? How?"

"That's what we have to figure out, but we're not alone. There are others. Free men and women."

III

Later, when the others had been liberated I was told of the fall-out from my escape. This was the story that was told to me:

"How did this happen!" screamed the facilitator. "You just let him walk out the door?"

The guard was intimidated, though he outsized her in every way. "He had on a lab coat and was looking through papers on a clip board. I thought he was one of you."

"You aren't hired to think!" The facilitator's face was crimson and the veins on her neck stood out. "From now on you will check everyone's identification. If they don't have an Institute ID with a photograph on it, you don't let them out!"

"How could *he* of all people get out," she muttered to herself, but loud enough that her assistant and the guard could hear. "He was – is – the most defiant of all the clients."

"I have notified the authorities and they have started a sea…"

She cut him off. "At least you did *something* right. I don't know what position could be lower than a guard at The Institute, but I'll find it and that will be your next post."

"The door to the supply room has had its lock jimmied," quietly said the assistant. "That's how he came to have a clip board. We searched his room and found a needle imbedded in the side of his mattress and several meters of white thread. Laundry says his sheets have come back with some of the material ripped off the bottom. That is how he fashioned a lab coat. It couldn't have been a very good one."

"Good enough for *him*," she spat, thrusting her index finger in the guard's chest. "I have a group session in five minutes, so everyone return to your duties. And *you*," she said glaring at the guard, "don't let anyone past you that doesn't have proper identification."

Strolling into the group session as elegantly as she could, she motioned for everyone to sit.

"Well, everyone is here. Martin is absent due to an illness. We had him transferred to the hospital for examination."

Some of the clients glanced at each other, a look that belied their doubts about the story they just heard. Everyone had heard the exchange between the facilitator and the guard and, so, knew that Martin's absence wasn't due to an illness. They had all been at the institute long enough not to outwardly challenge the facilitator.

"Who wants to begin? Tell us what you've learned."

"Did Martin's er, illness have anything to do with Timmy's release? They roomed together and were very close," asked one of the clients, his head tilted downward with a sideways glance.

The facilitator remained calm. "Well, the doctors are looking into that possibility, but they haven't made any determination yet. I would like us to focus on our behavior in society. How have you made decisions, since we last met, that reflects the objectives we have been discussing?"

"The last time I saw Martin – when we left our meeting – he looked fine. I could hear him and Timmy talking before Timmy left, but couldn't make out what they were saying. There have been rumors that Timmy has been seen on the grounds," said one other client.

"That is all we will talk about the disa…illness of Martin," she exploded. We will stay focused on behavior modification. If there is any more questions or comments about Martin, privileges will be suspended for the week. Is that understood?"

Everyone looked at the floor and, in unison, muttered their assent.

Because they had been in several of these sessions, each, in turn, uttered some platitude or other about getting along, respecting authority, and, in general, dicta on normative behavior. The session continued until the hour was over and they were dismissed.

The conversations on the way to their rooms – of those who were not timid about speaking – were filled with expressions of doubt about the "official" story.

"He got out, is what happened," said one.

"Escaped!" said another.

"Hey, what you guys talkin' about? Martin? Sure enough he buggered out. I would too if I could," said a third.

"All we need is a plan," offered the first one.

"Maybe we knock the guard and we're gone," was the advice of the second one.

"No. The guard'll knuckle us fer sure. He's too big. And now, he'll be on his guard like never before," said the third one.

"Let's think on it a spell. Maybe we can think of something." This from the first one.

They agreed to find a way – any way – to get out. With three minds like these, it'll be a cinch.

IV

After one of the people on the inside got a note to us, and after we formed a chain of correspondences, a plan was devised and a time set that Timmy and I would create a diversion. At the prescribed time, I walked into the main door of The Institute, up the stairs, and knocked on the glass panel of the door leading to the dormitory. The guard, still smarting from my escape looked at me with wide eyes.

"Martin!" he shouted as he opened the door.

I led him down the stairs, keeping him far enough away from catching me, yet close enough to keep up his hope of catching me. I led him down the stairs and out the door. I purposefully fell once to keep him close, then circled around the building where he could no longer see the door. Timmy got the others out; there were sixteen people.

Once I heard Timmy's whistle, I took off on a dead run, leaving the guard clutching his sides, panting.

We all met up later. We couldn't get everyone in Timmy's hut because there were too many people. Those others, "the others," Timmy spoke of took in everyone.

The difficulty we faced was how to bring the building down. We didn't like the facilitator, yet we didn't wish harm on her or anyone else.

It was summer. We could easily disable the air conditioners that were installed around the facilities. When the temperature inside the building became uncomfortable, everyone inside would have to evacuate. Besides they no longer had any "clients."

One of "the others" knew how the air conditioners worked, in fact had installed these very units. One night he cut the low voltage control wires from each of the air conditioners. He didn't just cut the wire, he told us, he removed several feet of wire so it wouldn't be a simple matter to fix them.

The next morning we noticed the facilitator, her assistant and the guard leave the building, locking the door as they left.

Some of us wanted to blow up the building with explosives. As much as I despised The Institute and what it represented, I wasn't in favor of violent means to bring it down. Others wanted to break in an open up the gas lines to cause an explosion.

"Look here," one of the former "clients" said, holding the paper.

Former Institute Director Jailed, was the headline. "The former director of The Institute was jailed this afternoon when it was found she was negligent in securing the clients of her facility. She will be tried for her dereliction and could be imprisoned for up to ten years." The story went on to report, "As a result of the escape of the clients of The Institute, the facility will be closed and the buildings razed. A new facility will be planned for the future."

"We don't have to destroy it," Timmy shouted. "They'll do it for us."

A cheer went up.

Yet we remained on the outside of society. If we were ever caught, we would be imprisoned, but not in anything like The Institute; we would be in a prison where there would be no hope of escape.

We live among you. We live in the shadows. You might find us seated at a table in a café, next to your table. You might pass us on the sidewalk or see us crossing the street alongside you.

We won't be assimilated into society; we can't be assimilated because we're outcasts. We're as much outcasts as if we were lepers. Believe me when I tell you, we aren't dangerous. We simply refuse to obediently defer to the commands of officials. We can disagree with vehemence. That is why we are where we are.

The Hanging

'Jake' Clanahan's life was one of challenges and struggles, trials nobody understood. Adrift, alone and living on his wits, he murdered one of Duley, Wyoming's honorable citizens and thus leads to the final episode in his tragic life.

I

May 12, 1887 - The hollow echo quieted the murmur of those observing the proceeding. A rare event in the southern Wyoming town of few inhabitants, a hanging brought all the men and most of the women and children. The thud of the trap door changed the tenor of the crowd. No longer were there taunts or laughter. Or jokes. Rather there was stillness from the men; the mouths of children hung gaping; and sniffles and tears among the women were plentiful.

The condemned, Thomas 'Jake' Clanahan, had been duly tried and convicted of the wanton murder of the proprietor of Duley, Wyoming's mercantile store. Why? Why had this happened to one of the townspeople's finest? Certainly it wasn't over a debt, since Jake Clanahan had never met Clyde Beckam, much less traded in his store. No it wasn't that at all. It was something else, something the sheriff, the judge, the jury and the townspeople couldn't understand. Jake just walked into the store and shot poor Clyde, leaving his wife, Hannah, a widow with four children to raise.

<>

August 3, 1880 - The trail was hard, hot and dusty. As far north as here in Montana the summer heat was stifling. The trail ride from Kansas took longer than expected; the six month drive was delayed by torrents at the Platte River, which swept some of the cattle to their deaths. These longhorns were not destined for Armour's Chicago packing plant; these were going where there was no easy rail routes.

Jake took on with the drive in Abilene. Out of work and out of money, at least he would be paid for his labors – not to mention being fed along the way. The work was hard, but Jake was familiar – even comfortable – with life's vicissitudes. Raised by a cruel widower and ordered to part ways at fourteen, Jake had been made to be tough; he was glad to be gone as the frequent beatings and fights had made the choice of being alone preferable to life with his father, a man who had treated Jake as if it was he – Jake – who was responsible for, and took an active part in, the death of his mother during child birth. From job to job, employer to employer, cheated and swindled, Jake learned to take what he could by whatever means he could. He would work a full day for a full day's pay, but would rob, cheat or steal if he felt he was dealt wrong. The trail bosses were hard but honest; a drover got his wages at the end of the drive; that was as good a surety as he had ever experienced.

The drive concluded, a beer and a bath – in either order – was called for. He didn't need the attentions of the saloon women. His past experiences had taught him not to trust 'em. Their attentions were designed to separate a herder from his pay, often by stealing it but as often in cahoots with a local tough to beat it out of someone. The sheriff did a minimal amount to restrict this, knowing those driving the steers up from the south would be gone soon enough.

Jake was tired. And hurting. Between being caught between two steers and thrown to the ground; beaten by a wild muleskinner that came with the drive back in Texas; and being hit with the butt of a rifle by the wagon master when it was thought he had fallen asleep while on watch, Jake felt every vein in his neck and scalp. Sometimes he forgot the people he worked with; he could see the features of their faces, but couldn't *see* their faces. He knew Luke, the cook, by the ever present cigar in his mouth – some said the ashes were his "special ingredient." Will was the tallest man he'd ever seen; he knew Will. The rest he didn't recognize. And everyone thought him crazy for not remembering folks he'd ridden with for twenty-nine weeks. The butt to his right temple and the kicks to his forehead must surely have damaged Jake, they all said. And they had. Recurring headaches, moments he just blacked out, and the voices. The time at the end of the drive would be a welcome respite.

II

May 12, 1887 - Some of the church folks donated to his burial. Jake got the best funeral six dollars and two bits would buy. The preacher, Reverend Ben Dilworth, duly performed the grave side service. Nobody else was there.

The sheriff kept Jake's gun. And his boots. The boots were worn with a hole in the right one and a loose heel on the left one. The gun wasn't much, the kind any trail man would own. It didn't exhibit the filing and polish of a gun slinger's weapon; it was just...a gun, and had a holster whose belt had exactly two bullets. The two bits he had in his pocket helped defray the cost of his funeral. Hannah Beckam received the proceeds from the sale Jake's horse and saddle.

His possessions were as much a mystery as his actions. Jake had little of his own and was seen staring into the Duley, Wyoming street – looking beyond the dirt, maybe someplace deep under the street – before entering Mr. Beckam's store. Trance-like, Jake raised his gaze from the street, walked across the street, into the store and put one bullet in Clyde's forehead. Why he nearly knocked over the people passing on the wooden sidewalk as he went in! Lou Redmond, in town buying supplies, was in the store, watched with his own eyes the killing, and jumped Jake holding him down until the sheriff arrived. Not a word was uttered by the killer, not when he was subdued, not when he was locked up, not when he was tried and not when he was hanged. A mystery. The Casper Sentinel did a piece on the whole matter; perhaps one day in the very distant future someone will understand. Nobody in 1887 could comprehend what happened.

III

September 1, 1880 – Missoula wasn't much more than a town at the edge of the mountains. The Army post contracted for the cattle that was brought north and, with the trail ride complete and money in his pocket, Jake was ready to move on. Besides, it was said, winter would soon come and with it bitter cold. Moreover, on this side of the mountains air movements brought snow, lots of snow; sometimes the snow could bury a man, they said.

With his saddle bag strapped to his horse and a few supplies, Jake set off. He wasn't sure where he was going, only that he would keep the sun ahead of him and on his left in the morning and to the right in the afternoon. He didn't much care to go any faster than the fifteen miles a day it took to get to Montana. Steady and south was his aim. Eventually he made his way into Wyoming, then Colorado, and finally wintering in Amarillo.

He spent two years working at the JA ranch outside Amarillo, working for John Adair and Charles Goodnight. Unafraid of hard work, Jake broke horses and mended fences; the cattle always seemed to push over fence posts and destroy the barbed wire. Too many times Jake was thrown from a horse, sometimes taking a blow to the head. When his actions became inexplicable – uncontrolled laughter, the sounds he claimed to be hearing, the incoherent babbling – he was fired. He became a man with no one to talk to and nowhere to be. Wandered around Texas and New Mexico Territory, time took on no meaning for Jake. It was in the spring of 1887 that Jake began to travel north.

<>

Travelling north through Utah Territory, Jake took exceptional pleasure in seeing the snow covering the mountains. Perhaps he was as happy as he could ever remember. Perhaps the most coherent thing he had said in the past seven years, nobody would hear.

"This is beautiful. I feel good!"

Jake put down for the night there. The mountains looked enormous and distant, yet seemed as if he could reach a hand out and take hold of them. There being sufficient small game, Jake spent a week there. He was never happier than in that week.

Until the headaches began – again. And the visions. Treacherous, evil images. Every bush was peering at him; every critter snarled. He closed his eyes tightly and pressed his hands against them but the images would persist. And so, he packed his things, what little remained, and went north. Soon he passed the two log cabins that were Fort Bridger. At the foothills of the Uinta Mountains, he found Duley. Not much of a town, really, maybe six stores on each side of the only street running North-South and two streets running East-West. A church that served as a school, a livery, a seamstress, a hotel, a saloon and Mr. Beckam's mercantile store were the only places of significance.

As Jake rode into town, he came to a halt across from Beckam's store, and slid, more than dismounted, from his horse, his vision blurred by the constant throbbing at his temples. He sat on the wooden step leading from the dirt road to the sidewalk and wiped his face with his shirt sleeve. Standing, he peered into – *into* – the dirt road.

"Hey, mister. You all right?"

Nothing.

"Friend, can I help you?"

More nothing.

"What's wrong with you? Are you drunk?"

Nothing.

Then he walked, trance like, across the street.

And, well, you know the rest. Jake's was a hard, tough life. He was shaped and formed by circumstances, the cruelties of this life. He wasn't hard, exactly; just made hard. Too many bumps and knocks – too many of those to his head. It would take years for the understanding to catch up and explain what happened to

Jake, but in his lifetime there was nobody that knew him – really *knew* him – and knew what he'd been through. Jake needed help that wasn't available and we can only lament this fate and the fate of the Beckam family and those who knew them.

Angie: The Roaring Romance

Their romance was quick, deep and torrid, yet it seemed it was over before it really began. All their plans were dashed and all that remained were his memories.

Angie came into my life suddenly, just as she had left me. She was vivacious, slender and tall. She had brilliant green eyes and slightly red hair. When she tilted her head back it was electric. Her laugh was gay and bright. All the world seemed to be hers and she was my gal.

We spend all our time together, often dancing and partying at Sean Donally's speakeasy on the south side. The bands were top-notch and the liquor was plentiful even in the midst of prohibition.

I grew up with Sean and we were everywhere together until we turned fourteen. Sean took a job with one of the Irish mob bosses in Hyde Park running errands and collecting money. When the Volstead Act was passed he was promoted to operating one of the speakeasies. He could be a tough character, Sean. If someone got out of hand it was pretty common for Sean to take the gent out back and rough the guy up. His reputation alone kept the place pretty orderly.

I met Angie at the club that October. She was wearing a beaded evening dress that hung close to her lithe body and a cloche hat that matched her dress. Her shoes were strap heeled shoes that matched the hat. She drew a lot of attention from the gents, let me tell ya. She would embrace them and kiss them on the cheek; every man wanted her but none could have her. She was elusive.

I was just out of the University of Chicago with an accounting degree working for Calumet National Bank. I'm tall and of average looks; smart both academically and street wise. I grew up in a wealthy family with a maid, a butler and a chauffeur and was reared to be a proper gentleman. I was all of that, let me tell ya.

For some reason Angie gravitated to me. Everyone it seems bought her drinks just for the chance to be near her. She saw something in me that I couldn't understand.

"C'mon, let's dance."

She teased me with a wink of her eye. I was surprised to be sure and not a little intimidated.

"I don't know."

"C'mon. It'll be fun.

"I'm, uh, ok just watching."

"You'll have more fun dancing," she said laughing and grabbing me by the hand.

She pulled me to the dance floor and we danced. She kept me on the floor most of the night. I don't mind telling you I was stiff at first. The drinks and Angie, however, loosened me up. We had a swell time. I laughed more than I had ever laughed before.

After the place closed she took me to her place. Her aroma aroused me more than I thought possible. For the first time in my life I felt unrestrained. I took her with a fervor I didn't know I had. Afterward we lay together drenched from sweat and feeling alive yet drained. Something in me was awakened and I wasn't sure if I should revel in it or be frightened. I pushed it out of my mind and rode its wave.

We ate at Berghoff's that afternoon. I was hungry; Angie ate very little.

"Aren't you hungry?"

"I don't eat much. I never have, at least as long as I can remember."

"You should eat. You need to keep up your strength."

We walked through Washington Park then went to a matinee. *The General* was showing. Angie and I laughed at Buster Keaton because he had a funny walk that was comical.

We went back to Washington Park, sat and talked. She was also from Hyde Park, born into a wealthy family. When I think of it, it's funny that we both had similar backgrounds yet were so different. She was so adventurous and I was so reserved. When we were together I felt different, less stilted and more relaxed. I began to walk around in my suit with one hand in my suit pocket and a cigarette in the other. I never would have done that before I met her.

Back at the club we had a terrific time. We became the center of attention because Angie always had us on the dance floor. Over the weeks and months that followed we were inseparable and recognized by everyone as a couple.

Then in mid-November I saw Angie using cocaine for the first time. She transformed from being nearly lethargic to being energetic in an instant.

"What is that, Angie?"

"It's cocaine. Try some."

"No! Don't do that. I don't like you to use that."

"Dearest, it makes me feel so alive! I can do anything. I'm ready to dance," she said as she twirled in place. "You have to get ready. It's almost six. I wanna dance." Her tone was stern.

"Ok. Ok."

Quick as I could I got ready. It was half past six when we left her place and drove to Sean's. We were there an hour when a bell sounded.

"What's that?" I was frantic not knowing what was happening.

Sean was nonplussed. "It's the alarm. The feds are coming. Behind the bar is a stairway to the cellar. Get going."

We ran to the back of the bar and followed the help down to the cellar. From there we walked through a tunnel that came out in the basement of a bakery. We ascended the stairway into the bakery, then out the back door. Sean locked the door. He didn't seem upset by all this.

"They'll smash everything."

"Sean, you'll be ruined."

Sean and I were leaning against the alley wall of the bakery. He handed me a smoke and then broke into laughter.

"How can you laugh?"

Angie joined in the laughter.

"The feds'll bust up the place all right. In a couple of days it'll be open again."

"What?" I stammered.

"She's right. I make enough on this joint that this is only a mild setback. In three days I'll be open again, four at the most. Let's go find a drink."

We walked the twelve blocks to another of Patrick Reilly's clubs. Mr. Reilly was there that night and Sean explained what had happened.

"The feds'll bust it up, Sean, and we'll replace everything. You'll be back in business in no time. It's good that you got out."

"I wasn't worried, boss. I figure we'll be back in business in a few days.

I was taking this in. It was only business when the feds busted up the place.

Right away, Angie wanted to dance. Being this was Mr. Reilly's prime club the music was better and the band was bigger. We danced until the place shut down the next morning. Before we left she made a stop in the restroom. "I'll be right back, dearie; I'm going to powder my nose."

She walked to the restroom with a heavy stride, slow like. In less than a minute she came out.

"Whey! I'm ready. C'mon, let's go."

Her eyes were wide and she had a walk that was more like dancing. Graceful. I looked at her and knew she had gone to the bathroom for some cocaine. She was transformed.

We took a cab to Henrici's on Randolph Street. Though it was early morning, they were still serving. We ate, then went to her place and made love. It was always terrific. We never tired of having each other and it was never routine. We always slaked our appetite for each other.

The wind blew off Lake Michigan fiercely that fall. November's temperature plummeted. Not to be deterred we donned our fur lined coats and carried on. Sean's club was shut down for four days after the raid and the shelves were restocked and things returned to normal.

The president of Calumet National came into the club and was surprised to see me. We pledged to each other not to mention our presence in Sean's place.

"Uh, oh, hi. I'm surprised to see you here."

"Me too, boss. I mean, surprised to see you here."

"What brings you here?"

"I come here occasionally."

"Look, uh, I'm gonna get myself a drink. I'll see you at work.

I think it was a benefit to me that I knew something about him he didn't want anyone else to know as he was especially friendly with one of the girls at the club. It wasn't exactly romantic but they were getting' close, if you know what I mean. I got a ten cent raise that next week.

A chill fell over Chicago that winter. Even by Chicago standards it was brutal. We didn't care, Angie and me. We took everything that came at us and gave it right back.

When the first snowfall came in early December we threw snowballs at each other. She took special delight when she would wind up like Ted Lyons then hit me in the back as I spun to avoid her throw. To be honest everything about her throw was comical, but I would always fall in the snow and pretend I was mortally wounded. It was a swell time and I always aimed to miss her.

We had great plans for Christmas. We planned to be married and booked a honeymoon cruise to South America. Our destinations were Rio and Buenos Aires on the east coast; Quito and Santiago on the west coast.

We would have made wonderful memories that Christmas. We were to fly to New York then take a ship to the east coast of South America, spend two weeks, pass through the locks of the Panama Canal to the west coast. I planned on taking my vest pocket Autographic camera to record the memories.

Sean congratulated us and threw a huge wedding for us at the club in early December. All the regulars knew us and wished us all the best. This was a grand event. Mayor Dever even attended and congratulated us, hoping our trip to South America was a swell one.

In late December I fell ill and was bed-ridden for most of the week. Angie took good care of me. She was terribly worried for me. We were days away from our honeymoon.

"You have to get better before we leave."

"I'm getting better. I was up and around this morning. I think I'll be all right." My fever had broken and I was gaining my strength.

Two days before Christmas Angie, drunk and tired, collapsed on a Chicago sidewalk. She never awakened.

I buried her at Oak Woods on Christmas morning. The brutal winter we defied had claimed its most wonderful victim.

Land Grab

Edward Kline lived on his land since 1896, raised a family and buried his wife on the property. When his land is suddenly of interest to men who wish to buy it, he is curious. Neighbors of his have received the same offer and he sets out to determine the nature of the interest in the land around Albuquerque, New Mexico.

Two men rode the dirt path to Edward Kline's farm house in 1945, right after V-J Day and wanted to buy his land. Both men were tall, clean shaven and wore dark suits. They claimed they'd give him top dollar for all hundred acres. They'd been to the court house and seen the abstract so they knew exactly what land was Edward's.

"No. I've got my will prepared and filed with my lawyer. The land's going to my boys."

"Who's your lawyer?" one of the men asked.

"Well, now, you don't need to know that." Edward was becoming perturbed.

"We know your boys aren't around. We can wait till you're gone and buy it from them for a lot less than we're offering you," said the other one.

"My boys, at least one of 'em will take over once I'm gone. I know that sure as anything. Even though they're gone now, they'll come back." Edward was becoming more agitated as the conversation wore on.

"Look, Mr. Kline, you've toiled your entire life," the first one said as he shielded his face from the sun with his hand. "With what we're willing to pay, you can buy a nice house in town and rest. You've earned that for yourself."

"And who knows, at your age you could easily fall and hurt yourself. Then who'd take care of the place? You got no family here abouts."

"Me and ma bought this place in '96 and worked it and made a life here. She's buried out next to the house. See that little fence?" he said as he pointed with a nod of his head. "She's buried inside that fence."

"We're sorry for your loss," they replied together.

"You think about it for a while and we'll be back to talk about it again," said the first one. He left a business card that said he represented New Mexico Development Company.

Not two days later two other men came with the same offer; top dollar, they said, same as the first fellows. They weren't as tall as the first two but they dressed as nice as the others; one had a mustache and sun glasses, the other was clean shaven with sun glasses. They had been to the court house same as the first couple had. Their card said Southwest Development Corporation.

In both cases, Edward thought, nobody said what "top dollar" meant and why his land was so valuable. If he sold, Edward would have to have his wife's body removed to one of the cemeteries in town; he didn't wish to do that. But he couldn't understand the sudden interest in his land.

Edward Kline owned a hundred acres in New Mexico, not that it was terribly productive land. No, it was scrub land barely suitable for the eighty steers he owned. Edward, born in 1875 in Louisiana, was five feet seven, about three inches shorter than when he was in his twenties. His hair was mostly gone, which he covered with a straw hat; he wore coveralls and work boots except on Sundays when he wore his only suit and oxfords to go to church.

Edward's sons, Blake and Jacob left the farm in 1925 and '26 respectively. Blake went to Kansas City and Jacob took out for Des Moines, Iowa. They married local girls and tired of the hot summers working the farm. Edward got letters from the boys occasionally telling of his grandkids and life away from New Mexico. Once a year they'd send a family photograph that Edward treasured.

The man passed his idle hours sitting in his living room rocking chair next to the small table by the window, reading his Bible. Edward maybe knew the Bible more than the preacher did. He grew up reading it with his mother, Esther and it became a habit he never relinquished. The local pastor was a man named Jethro Tertullus Beachum; that first name was from Moses' father-in-law and the middle name was after the lawyer that attempted to prosecute the Apostle Paul in Governor Felix's court. He was the son – and grandson – of a preacher man. Knew his Bible, too, did the preacher. Maybe as much as Edward.

After the second couple of fellas visited Edward, he drove to his closest neighbor's house. William Horace Braken was a tall, muscular German immigrant who owned eighty acres and fifty head of cattle. His story mirrored that of Edward. Two pairs of men came with the same story: wanted to buy the land and would pay "top dollar." William showed identical business cards to those given to Edward. William had talked to other neighbors and received the same story. Some folks wanted this land real bad. Edward and William wanted to know the reason.

William hopped into Edward's truck, a 1940 Ford pickup. They drove into town and talked with folks at three banks.

"Mr. Cline. Mr. Bracken." The bank manager at Southwest Bank was a short bespectacled man of some years.

"Mr. Crenshaw, we've gotten offers for our land," Edward stated, "and, come to find out, so have a lot of folks around here. Can you tell what's going on?"

"No." The word was drawn out and the bank manager rubbed his chin. "I do know that them folks have been askin' a whole lot of folks about their land.

"Two pair of gents," William said.

"Yep. Two pair of men. One pair from Southwest Development Corporation and the other pair from New Mexico Development Company."

"That's them," said Edward.

"Nope. Don't know what's goin' on."

Others were asked about this an gave the same response – and nobody knew why the interest in the land.

Inquiries at several businesses netted some rumors and speculation, however no two stories were the same.

The most plausible explanation was that there was a proposed land development for older folks, a senior citizen development. That seemed probable. The most bazaar explanation was that the government was planning on building some military complex that would house people – if they can be called "people" – from outer space.

William and Edward returned to William's farm and sat with coffee to think the situation through. True enough, Roosevelt had died and Truman had become president. What did those facts have to do with anything? The war in Europe was won. Japan was bombed into submission and the troops returned home. So what?

The phone interrupted their thinking.

"Yeah. This is Bill," said William.

"Well, Edward and I was just talkin' about that as you called."

"Edward Kline."

"Well, truth be told, we can't figure it out either."

"Really? You sure?"

"Ok. I'll tell Edward. Don't know if that helps understand what's goin' on or not."

"Thanks. Goodbye."

William returned to the porch with the coffee pot and filled both cups. He sat down and explained the phone call.

"I don't know what to make of it but James Parker just called. Said he had heard that they found uranium in a coal mine recently. He says it's a 'radioactive' material and was important to the country and that Truman is interested in it. James says a government man has been around asking questions.

Edward took off his hat and scratched his head.

"Don't know what that is or why it's important. Don't know what it would have to do with our land.

"Don't ya see, Ed? If the government is interested in the uranium they might want to buy up land and built some kind of plant to use it to make bombs or for some other use. It'd make our land worth a lot of money. These developers buy the land from us and sell it to the government for a whole lot more than they'd pay us."

"Now I get it. Even 'top dollar' today wouldn't be as much as the government would pay for the land next week or next year."

"Right. I'm holding my land 'til the government makes an offer. I'm gonna be rich!" William beamed at the prospect of his yet-to-be acquired wealth.

After a moment of reflection, Edward agreed.

Well, William, Edgar, and the other land owners spurned the offers made by New Mexico Development Company and Southwest Development Corporation.

None of the land owners were made rich though; the government didn't buy their land.

Oh, the government was interested in the uranium all right and had plans to produce a hydrogen bomb in New Mexico. It just wasn't in that part of New Mexico, Albuquerque. They bought land in Los Alamos about ninety miles to the north.

Edward's son Jacob returned to the farm with his family when Edward fell and broke his hip in '69. His grandsons got the chance to know their grandpa before he died that summer. Jacob inherited the farm by himself as Blake expressed no interest in the land. The kids play around that fence and Jacob keeps the grass and the two graves in proper order. One more generations of Klines farm near Albuquerque. Perhaps the next generation will too. And who knows for how long.

Will's Dream

Will dreamed of life beyond his small village, of parades and circuses. His wanderlust took him to faraway places, to war, and to an ultimate yearning he never before realized.

The climb up the steep hill was challenging for Will's short legs and chubby stature. Will was determined because, he was told, from the summit one could see everything. A world awaited his vision and he was eager to venture beyond the small boundary that was his home and neighborhood. He knew – and loved – everyone in his village, but he knew that there was more, had to be more. The cobbler tap tapping away or the baker working, kneading, his bread or the banker at his cage, these were such common sites as to be nearly unseen by Will. Wasn't there more? Were there no circuses? No travelling shows? Bards? Minstrels?

And so he trudged, step by step. The summit seemed so far from him, as something nearly unattainable. Yet he continued. He had been a long time gone from home; when he began the sun was low in the sky and now it was nearly overhead. As the sun rose and he struggled against the incline, he began to sweat heavy drops of sweat. He knew, too, that there was one shade tree visible even from the bottom; that would provide him shade and afford an opportunity to cool himself. Would that he had remembered to bring water, he could further refresh himself.

Though it seemed like forever, Will reached the peak. He had to rest and catch his breath before looking across the expanse. When he did, he was dismayed. He saw one village in the distance that looked little different from his own. He saw fields of an ordinary kind, and pens wherein were cattle and sheep and pigs. There was nothing like he imagined, no tents or parades. Will sat under the tree, one of two on the summit, the other having been toppled by wind and erosion. He sat there and napped, dreaming of what might be beyond the horizon.

There he determined that, one day – he didn't know when – he would venture to places beyond which he could see from this vantage point. He wanted something different.

Later, when he was twenty and not so chubby and not so short legged, he was summoned by the gendarme for conscription into the army of the republic.

The presence of the gendarme was frightening and the entire family gathered at the door in response to his knock.

"I am here for Will," said he.

"What do you want with my son," his mother replied.

"Will and three others in the village are required for military service. They are to leave in the morrow for training."

"But…why my son?"

"It is required," was his only explanation.

For the first time in his young life, he left the village of his birth and found himself in a barracks some days walk from home. There he exercised and practice with a rifle and a knife. In a fortnight, he was transferred to learn cannonry. This was his post, to pack powder into the cannon and roll the shot into its mouth.

He and his fellow soldiers were loaded onto a train. They trudged along worn tracks to a point near the front. There they offloaded their things and moved to where others were fighting. The sounds were deafening. Will had only heard two cannons before this day. Now there were eight cannons firing nearly at the same time. No one knew if they struck anything; they fired, then reloaded, and fired again. All they could see of the enemy was puffs of smoke until once his forces were nearly overrun, and would have been if not for the cavalry that drove off the enemy. When Will saw these people – the enemy – he was shocked to see that they appeared no different than himself, or those of his small village. They – the enemy – were said to be of the worst kind, evil; he expected horns and claws, yet they were much as himself. They were young men – and scared, much as he was scared.

"There they are! Load the canons," cried the general. "Steady. Fire."

And the canons exploded.

"Who are these people?" Will asked.

The general's answer was crisp. "The enemy. Reload."

Turning to another soldier, Will whispered, "They look same as us."

"Fire!"

For four days the fighting continued and then the guns were silent. Most of the men knew nothing of why it ended, only that their commander ordered them to break camp and return to the railroad line. Will was mustered out of the army within a month. Upon discharge Will thought about returning to his village and was torn between greeting his family and striking out to find what he had pondered so long ago.

After some consideration, he realized that his village would be where it had always been and that he could return any time. So it was that he struck out along the rail line guessing it would lead to some place of adventure, that for which he searched on that hill some years earlier.

The rail line crossed rivers and canyons and along miles of fields until he arrived at a city unlike his village. It had stone and brick building, some as tall as three stories. There were building with arched entrances and windows with glass. He saw carriages with coverings over them, drawn by *two* horses. The few people in his village that had any horses only had one. There were no more than three horses in the entire village, one belonging to the gendarme and another belonging to the postmaster; the third horse belonged to the man who owned the bank. Here there seemed to be scores of horses and buggies or carriages.

He heard music from a building and peered inside. This was the first time he had seen a piano-forte; he knew what it was from picture books, but this was the first time he had seen or heard one. Therein were two women in long, shiny dresses walking from table to table, visiting with people seated there. Will was pushed inside as two old men entered.

"Here's to a drink, young fella," said one of them to Will.

"Just go to that man over there behind the bar and ask for a drink," said the other.

Will walked hesitantly to where the man was, not knowing what there was or what he wanted. The man behind the bar poured a stein full of beer and gave it to him, demanding one copper coin.

Will had never been drunk before – had never had a drink before – and when he awakened in the morning he found himself in an alley and his money was gone. His head hurt and his stomach was churning. He raised himself to his feet and steadied himself against the building. His walk was meandering and the least sounds hurt his head.

Soon he wandered to the blacksmith shop.

"Sir, can I find work with you? I'm young and strong."

"Well, what can ya do fer me?"

"Sir, I don't know anything about smithing, but I'm strong and I can learn."

"Fer two coppers a day you can keep my fire stoked and keep the place tidied up…and anything else I tell ya to do. You'll be paid end of each day. Agreed?

"Yes sir," Will replied. In a month he had earned enough to leave.

Will followed the railroad tracks. Soon he found a slow moving train and jumped on board. He was surprised to see other travelers there. One crowded him and wanted his money. The confrontation reached a climax when Will pushed the elderly man out the door of the train car and onto the rail bed.

In two weeks he saw the landscape change, looking like those fields he saw from the top of the hill. The fields were turning a golden color and the sky's blue color changed to that hue that signified fall and, soon enough, winter.

His journey took eighteen days and Will ended up where he began. His village looked so much different now and the first sounds he heard were the cobbler's hammer, a pleasant sound to his ears, actually.

The townspeople – the cobbler, the baker, and the banker – once so common, Will now cherished and found so dear.

Speedway

A chance encounter at one of Speedway's famous institutions forms a bond between to residents and, maybe, a lasting friendship.

I was having breakfast the other day at Charlie Brown's – ham and cheese omelet, hash browns, toast and coffee – when I ran into an old fellow from Speedway. I was seated at one of the two horseshoe counters – the one closest to the door. It was busy that day, much like any day, really, and all the booths and tables were full. The fellow next to me got up to leave and this man sat down.

"Hello, young man."

I looked around to see if he was really talking to me. I didn't think he was *that* much older than me.

"Hello. How are you?"

"Better'n I have a right to be. Just had my check up and I'm strong as a horse."

"You from…"

"Hey, Billy. You want the usual?" The waitress was skinny and maybe in her early 40's, wearing a maroon t-shirt with a checkered flag pattern around the midriff.

"Yeah. The usual. Over easy on the eggs." Billy was short and stocky, wore blue work pants and a red shirt with a button down collar. His head was bald on top with wisps of hair around his ears and he wore glasses with a black frame.

"You from around here?" I asked.

The counter, like all the booths had a faux marble top and brown seats. There was racing memorabilia everywhere. If a person was dropped in blindfolded, they'd know this was Speedway, Indiana.

It was early and the sun hadn't risen above the buildings on the other side of the street. We sat in the ambient light of the morning, ate and visited.

His was an interesting story. He told me that he grew up around the track and loved the sounds and smell of the cars. Well, seems as if when he was a young preteen he would work with the newspaper company to sell papers at the track. He tells me that he never sold any of those papers; he would pay the newspaper company for 'em then toss them in the trash can once he got in. Well, he told me, if you was the newspaper boy you'd get in for free.

He had seen all the great race car drivers, names you'd know and some not so familiar. Met some of 'em, too. All for the cost of a few papers – at a discount too!

Billy joined the Army and served our country, he did. Came back home, got a nice job working for Allison's and raised a family. They still live around here, the family. He only talked a little about his service, only that he was a corpsman; he only saw a little action "'cause this was after we pulled out of Viet Nam."

He married a sweet gal, he said, a girl he knew from high school. They had three children - two boys and a girl. Them kids is grown now and have families of their own he told me. He pulled out his wallet to show me the pictures. He didn't have any pictures on his flip phone 'cause he didn't understand how to use it, the phone – only to make and answer calls. Nice lookin' family too; wife was pretty and the kids were nicely dressed.

Well, I hadn't grown up here, I told him, but seeings how I lived only a mile and a half I could hear the cars. I've been to the track same's so many others and I've always enjoyed the scene. He smiled and nodded at my telling him this. I told him about my job working for the street department. I retired six years before and spent my time at the library and the Legion.

We didn't talk too much after his food came. That's just the way life is I suppose; the way we was raised: it's not polite to talk with your mouth full.

Behind us was the clatter of dishes being cleared from a table and put into a tub. I hadn't noticed much else in the restaurant other than the gentleman and the waitress. Now I saw a white haired man and an attractive older woman sitting at a booth. They talked all the while eating. Two young men sat on the opposite side of our horseshoe. Now there was a noticeable din about the place.

My new friend finished his food and we got more refills of coffee then talked some more.

I told him how it was I came to be here and about my family. I showed him pictures – on my smart phone since I knew how to operate it. He held my phone at arm's length, turned in one way, then the other and nodded.

"Nice," was all he said.

"Wait," I said as I swiped the phone with my finger to show him another picture.

He smiled when he saw my youngest grandson, a red-headed boy with a freckle-splotched face. "That one looks like he could be a handful."

"His momma says so," I replied.

Oh, Billy still goes to the track all right. Now, he said, he just pays the fare to get in. They got them boxes set up now where you can buy a newspaper. He was a bit peeved by that. How's a kid supposed to have any fun he asked. Now he and the whole family go to the track. Practices, qualifications and, of course, the race. They all go. He told me that there's the same excitement today as when he was that kid with the newspapers.

Well, about this time there was a line at the door and the waitress was shooing us out so we parted ways. A nice man, that fella. I hope I run into him again. I like to think he reflected the soul of Speedway.